Secre·

by
Paul J Jackson

Copyright © Paul J Jackson 2022

ISBN: 9798833516638

Cover design by: Paul J Jackson

Also available by Paul J Jackson

My Soul to Take

Down a Dark Path - Sinister Tales
of Supernatural Horror

Retribution

1

It began to rain as the coffin was lowered into the ground and Edward watched it disappear, as if being swallowed by a hungry, gaping, mouth.

"Bye dad!" he whispered, his eyes welled with tears.

From the moment he had learned of his father's murder, through the week at the orphanage and being asked questions by the other children, he had not shed a single tear. He had been so traumatised it had rendered him unable to think clearly or stay focussed, but now, as he watched the coffin sink below the grass, the penny dropped and the tears began to fall.

A terrible feeling of loneliness had overwhelmed him, the realisation of having no one left he loved to care for him was terrifying. He was all alone with no relatives to take him in and forced to go wherever the care system thought best.

For a moment, he found himself thinking of his mother, Heather. If anything, losing her had been even more traumatic and he felt a little guilty even thinking such a thing as he stood at the graveside. He knew that his tears were for her too.

She had died seven years earlier in a fire at her great aunt's house but before that had been missing for almost a week. His father had always blamed himself for her leaving them because they had argued the day before she left.

Her coffin was now below his father's in the same dirty hole and the headstone had been taken away to have the inscription amended. He was too young back then to even wonder why she had been buried, being half cremated already and all, but it did feel strange seeing it dug open again, wrong even, as if they were exposing her or disturbing her privacy.

The memory of her drying his hair as he got ready for bed was the last one Edward had. He was pulling faces at her through the mirror and she was laughing and joking. She was happy and was not acting like someone about to leave her son but, when he woke the next morning, she was gone.

There was no note to explain why and none of her clothes had been taken. It was completely out of character and remains a mystery to this day. Her passing had broken his heart and he had never fully recovered from it. Like his father's death, hers had been a complete shock, a kick in the guts that had taken a while to sink in. To say he was devastated when it finally did would be a massive understatement.

A heavy hand being placed on his shoulder jolted Edward from his thoughts and he quickly wiped away his tears. Mr Carter, his dad's long time friend and employer was now standing at his side.

The man had handled all the funeral

arrangements on behalf of Edward and had paid for the service. The congregation was made up of a dozen strangers Edward had never seen before. Mr Carter, his wife, and a man called DaSilva were the only members of the group that he recognised.

DaSilva had worked with his father but they had not been close friends. On the four or five times he had met the man, Edward had sensed an air of tension between them, a kind of uneasiness. He had hardly ever spoken in Edward's presence but he had heard enough to know he was foreign. DaSilva had only ever looked at him disdainfully, as if Edward had wronged him somehow. He disliked the man immensely and he knew that the feeling was mutual.

Mr Carter handed Edward a single rose and then guided him towards the grave. Edward knew what he was supposed to do with it, he had seen it in a movie once, but he hesitated as he looked down upon the coffin.

The hole was not as deep as he was expecting and he could see the rain drops quivering on the polished lid. There was a brass plaque in the centre and the lettering, that was etched into it, had begun to fill with water.

Edward read the short inscription to himself.

"In loving memory of Gareth Kane 1923 to 1961".

His father had not long turned thirty eight and the brass plaque cruelly reinforced the reality that he was gone and that Edward would never see him again. He became transfixed on the name plate and froze.

Mr Carter, sensing the boys reluctance, gave him a nudge and, by reflex action alone, Edward threw the rose into the grave. It fell lifelessly onto the coffin lid and dislodged a solitary petal.

For some reason, after the rose hit the casket, Edward glanced towards DaSilva. He did not believe the story he had been given regarding the way his dad had died. He felt that DaSilva had something to do with it, or at the very least, should have been able to prevent it. Perhaps he just wanted to see DaSilva's face, his expression. Was he sad, happy or indifferent? For whatever reason it was, Edward felt compelled to look at him.

At first, DaSilva's eyes widened slightly as he saw the boy looking but, as he realised that the glance was not a friendly one, they slowly narrowed to menacing slits. Sophia, Mrs Carter, tipped her umbrella to one side, tapping DaSilva on the head with one of the spokes and Edward looked away before he attracted any more attention.

Edward's father had worked for William Carter for years and had become one of his closest friends. Mr Carter was a wealthy businessman who owned a successful haulage and shipping company.

Gareth had helped run the business and, along with DaSilva, would often be sent to retrieve money from people unwilling to pay their bill. Edward had been told that his father had been killed whilst trying collect a debt.

He was also told that the man, Charles Walker, had then taken his own life in front of DaSilva but the story did not ring true for Edward. Why did the man let DaSilva live? He had just killed his father but then decided to commit suicide and leave a witness, it was unbelievable.

He felt that DaSilva was lying about what really happened. He had no idea why, and he could not prove it, but he was determined to find out the truth, even if it took him the rest of his life to do it.

Once Mr Carter had thrown his rose onto the coffin he guided Edward back into the congregation of strangers. Edward's care worker, Ruth Meadows, had arrived and was there waiting for him behind the group of people. She was a large black lady with big yellowed eyes and shiny cheeks.

"Has he been told!?" inquired Mr Carter.

Ms Meadows looked at Edward and smiled awkwardly.

"Not yet!" she answered looking back at Mr Carter "I thought it would be best coming from you, you know, a familiar face an'all"

Edward looked at Ruth and asked her what they were talking about. She had visited him many times at the orphanage and he was beginning to trust her, feel comfortable with her.

Ruth smiled sympathetically at him as she sensed his anxiety building and began to talk but was interrupted by Mr Carter.

"As your father was a good friend of mine I've

arranged for you to come and stay with me under the care of Miss Roberts, our kitchen assistant."

Edward shook his head. He had been expecting to return with Ruth and stay at the orphanage indefinitely. He had started to make a few friends and the possibility of staying with Mr Carter had never occurred to him.

"But I want to stay where I am" he said, grabbing Ruth's hand.

The thought of spending part of his life with the same people he held responsible for his father's death appalled him. At this point he wanted nothing more than to distance himself from them.

"Nonsense boy!" snorted Mr Carter "Everything has been arranged!"

"Ruth!?" pleaded Edward.

Ms Meadows sighed "I'm sorry Edward but Mr Carter is right, everything has been arranged!"

"But, don't I get to choose who I live with?"

Ruth pulled Edward towards her, resting his head on her large breasts, and explained to him that she was only a temporary care worker and that she would soon be looking after another child in similar circumstances.

"As soon as we find you a foster home or guardian to live with my job is done!" she added.

Edward pushed himself away from her angrily, he had not considered himself as her job before. He could not believe that all her kindness and affection had all been false and that she was simply doing her job. Could he trust no one?

"Edward!" exclaimed Ruth, nearly toppling back as Edward pushed away.

Although he was only thirteen Edward was already quite tall and strong.

"Don't be angry, surely you realised you'd be re-homed at some point?"

Saying nothing, Edward turned to face Mr Carter. If even the kindest of people could not be trusted then he may as well stay with those who were untrustworthy, at least he would not let his guard down and be disappointed.

Edward was smart. It was obvious to him that he had no choice about where he was going to stay, or with whom, so he quickly set about smoothing is way back into Mr Carter's good books. After all, he did want to know the truth about his father's death and where better to do that than within the lion's den.

"I'm sorry for sounding ungrateful," he said, stepping closer, "it's just that its come as a surprise. I would be happy to stay with you!"

He held out his hand and Mr Carter shook it, just as Edward had hoped.

"Now that's more like it boy!"

Sophia had been watching them talking. She had kept her distance from them and was clearly not happy about what she was witnessing. Edward could see her speaking to DaSilva through the corner of her mouth, communicating inconspicuously.

2

Before long, Edward was travelling back to the Carter Estate in a black limousine that was being driven by a man he recognised from his family photographs. He had served in the army with his father and Edward was sure his name was Connor.

He had not attended the service, and had stayed near the limo during the burial, but did smile and nod at Edward as he opened the door for the party to get in.

Edward felt uncomfortable and somewhat out numbered as he sat looking out of the window. He was sitting next to DaSilva and facing Mr Carter, Sophia was sat next to her husband and facing DaSilva.

He felt as though all eyes were on him and was reluctant to take his gaze from the window but was eventually forced to as Mr Carter addressed him. Edward was told that Miss Sarah Roberts, the assistant cook, was to be his new guardian and that he would stay in the servants' quarters with her.

It was made quite clear that Edward was not to be treated, or accepted, as one of Mr Carter's family, more a temporary member of staff until he was sixteen and old enough to make his own decisions.

As Mr Carter gave him that piece of

information, Edward glanced briefly at Sophia. She was looking down at the rings on her fingers as she adjusted them. He wanted to see her reaction to what was being said but she appeared bored and uninterested. Something about her persona felt odd as he watched her. He couldn't put his finger on it but there was something.

He would be schooled one day a week and would work for his keep the rest of the week by assisting the grounds man with chores around the estate. The weekends would be his own.

"Do you understand Edward?"

"Yes sir." replied Edward, nodding.

He was sure DaSilva was looking at him, he could feel his cheeks reddening as his eyes burned into his skin. He wanted to look at him but knew it would create a scene.

Mr Carter continued to explain the rules of living at the Estate, a place he proudly referred to as 'The Manor House'. Edward was warned that he must not approach anyone from the Manor House and must not speak to anyone unless spoken to first.

Again he was asked if he understood and , with a nod of the head, the rules continued. He was not to venture into the Manor House unaccompanied and he was to do as he was told at all times.

"I know it sounds like I'm treating you badly Edward, but I'm not. I'm simply keeping your feet on the ground and making sure you're aware of your place in the big scheme of things, that's all."

Edward had almost stopped listening and just nodded approvingly once in a while but then Sophia suddenly interrupted, taking him by surprise.

"For god's sake William," she said, rolling her eyes, "couldn't you have told him all this later? You're boring me."

She spoke with a slight accent, Edward had guessed it was Spanish but couldn't be certain. It was very similar to how DaSilva spoke but less pronounced. Mr Carter, also taken aback at his wife's interruption, looked at her sternly.

"I won't have time later and the boy needs to know his place."

"His place was in the children's home," she scoffed.

Mr Carter sat glaring at Sophia for an uncomfortably length of time before speaking again. It was clear she had embarrassed him.

"His place is where I say it is." he growled.

Fortunately for Edward, nothing more was said for the rest of the journey and he felt he could have cut the atmosphere with a knife.

Edward could not understand Sophia's dislike towards him. Although they had only met a handful of times and had not really spoken to each other he had done nothing to warrant such hostility. She had been friends with his mother just like William, Mr Carter, had been friends with his father.

She would pull up outside their house in her car from time to time and pip the horn. His mother would run out to greet her and they would speed off somewhere together for a couple of hours leaving Edward with a baby sitter.

On the odd occasion when she spotted him looking at her through the window she had waved at him but had never smiled. To him, Mrs Carter, had always appeared 'doll like' with her shiny make-up and bright red lips.

He had not seen her since his mother's death seven years previously but could see that she had not changed, still hidden behind a cosmetic mask and unable to smile.

At last, they had arrived. The gravel crunched under the wheels as they cruised along the driveway and soon the large Manor House towered above them. The driveway was bordered by low walled flowerbeds and a fountain, a statue of cupid, served as a small round-about to the front of the building.

It was an imposing stately home with a central stone portico on a raised stepped plinth and the facade of the building was covered almost entirely in creeping vines of green and red. Many of the numerous windows, that were flanked by wooden shutters, were also hidden behind the foliage.

Directly above the portico were three slender arched windows, a tall one in the middle with shorter ones to either side and all were glazed with stained glass - the picture of a sunset spanning all three windows.

As the limousine pulled along side the portico a man in a black suit stepped out from beneath it and opened the door. The sky was still black with clouds but the sun was beginning to burn through.

Sophia was first to exit followed by Mr Carter and then DaSilva. Reluctantly, Edward stepped down from the vehicle onto the gravel drive, dragging his holdall with him.

Mounting the few steps, Sophia turned to him with an odious smile and said that she hoped Edward would soon settle in. It was obviously a fake gesture and done only to please her husband. DaSilva simply nodded in his direction before making his way towards the entrance.

"This is Edward Kane, the boy I told you about." said Mr Carter, addressing the man who had greeted them.

"Edward, this is Albert, head of staff. He will show you to your room."

The man smiled and shook hands with Edward courteously as Mr Carter continued to speak.

"Take the weekend to settle in and meet the staff and Sarah will guide you from there. Have you got any questions?"

Edward thought for a moment. He wanted so much to ask if he had killed his father, or at least, knew the truth but, instead, he shook his head.

"No, Mr Carter, I don't think so."

"In that case, I have things to do ." And with

that, Mr Carter smiled at Edward, nodded at Albert and made his way into the house.

Albert, an elderly man with grey hair, spoke to the driver briefly before asking Edward to follow him. Again, the driver acknowledged the lad with a friendly nod and Edward obliged him with a smile before following the old man inside. Mr Carter had already disappeared by the time they had entered the house.

Edward followed Albert across the large cold hallway, with its polished parquet flooring and grand central staircase, and through a door which eventually led left to the kitchen via a long corridor that was lit by wall mounted lamps and several long narrow, Georgian wired, roof windows.

The place had a smell to it that reminded Edward of his old school hall, damp and woody, and the air felt almost as cold as outside in places.

"So, you're Kane's boy?" asked Albert as they walked along the corridor.

Edward nodded. "Yes."

"A good man. I'm am sorry for your loss."

"Thank you."

The old man had sounded quite sincere but then his tone changed.

"I trust Mr Carter has explained your standing here?"

"Standing?"

Without warning, Albert stopped in his tracks and grabbed Edward by the arm, forcing him to face him.

"Your place boy, your position. I hope you understand it?" he said sternly.

Edward looked confused. The man suddenly appeared quite menacing.

"Although your father was held in high regard around here, you are at the bottom of the pecking order and will not be given any special privileges."

Edward could see this for what it was. The old man was trying to stamp his authority over him from the start and establish a dominant stance. He wanted Edward to know that he gave the orders to the lower ranks and he was expected to obey.

He was far from being afraid of Albert but knew that now was not the time to show it. His father had always told him to never let anyone push him around, no matter who they were, and had taught him how to protect himself very well. He knew the old man wouldn't stand a chance if he were to erupt, however, he felt that this was a time to show restraint and bite his lip.

"I'm in charge." added the old man.

"I understand." said Edward, glaring back into Albert's eyes.

They both stared at each other for a short while without blinking but it was Albert who was forced to turn away. His eyes had begun to water and his cheeks had reddened slightly, he was clearly annoyed at losing. Without another word he led Edward into the kitchen.

3

The kitchen was a large rectangular room with an uneven flagstone floor. There were two large coal fired stoves directly ahead of Edward as he entered and a small window with a door, that led out to a courtyard, to his left. A sturdy wooden table stood in the centre of the room with items of cutlery strewn across it, along with a large bowl of flour, and several chairs tucked in around it. The scent of roast lamb hung thick in the air.

Edward could see two women with their backs to him preparing vegetables as he entered. They both turned round together as they heard the door creaking to a close. One was an elderly woman with blotchy skin and a red nose and the other was a strawberry blonde with flour on her cheeks. The latter was obviously Miss Roberts.

Edward smiled awkwardly as their eyes met. "This is Edward Kane." said Albert, addressing the two women as he made his way around the table.

"Edward, this is Mrs Holland, the head cook, and Miss Roberts, her assistant and your new guardian."

"Pleased to make your acquaintance young man," said Mrs Holland, unceremoniously pushing passed him with a bucket full of vegetables.

She didn't appear to be very happy that he was there. Perhaps she too was showing him who was in charge around here. Edward quickly stepped aside to let her through. Sarah, however, seemed genuinely pleased to see him. She quickly wiped her hands down her pinafore and neatened her hair.

"It's nice to meet you, Edward," she said, shaking his hand, "I was sorry to hear about your pa."

Edward simply smiled and gave a small grateful nod.

"Are you hungry?" she asked.

"Starving."

She told him to take a seat while she fetched him some food.

"We're just preparing the evening meal for the house and I have nothing else to offer you." she explained, as she placed a tray of bread and cheese in front of him.

Edward smiled. "That's fine. I like bread and cheese."

"I'll see if I can keep you a bit of lamb for later," she said, passing him a cheese knife, "something nice for supper."

"Don't be too soft on the lad, Sarah," snorted Mrs Holland, transferring the vegetables into a large pot of boiling water, "You'll do him no favours by mollycoddling."

"But he's just buried his father, surely he's entitled to a little kindness?"

"He'll eat whatever we give him, don't let him think he has a choice."

Sarah chuckled and sat down beside Edward.

"Don't mind her," she whispered, "she's like that with everyone."

Edward thought not. She resented him being here just as much as the old man did. Albert, who by now was also sitting down, butted in.

"Anne's right," he said, "The boy needs to know his place from the beginning. I've just told him that myself outside."

"And the sooner he accepts it the better." added Mrs Holland.

As if encouraged by Mildred's input, Albert continued. "He has to come to terms with the fact that he's at the bottom of the pecking order around here."

Edward picked up a piece of bread and tore it in two.

"Don't worry," he said, taking a bite, "I heard you the first time."

Albert's eyes narrowed. "What was that?" he sneered.

"I said that I'm not deaf. How many times are you going to tell me that I'm the lowest of the low? I got it first the time, old man."

Sarah gasped at the remark and Mrs Holland stopped what she was doing and turned to face Edward. Her mouth had dropped open and she appeared shocked, as if he had committed some terrible crime.

Albert stood up sharply and sent the chair screeching across the floor.

"Watch you tongue, boy." he snarled, "I could have you flogged."

Edward was finding it hard to show restraint and bite his lip. The old man looked hell bent on making his life a misery and Edward was beginning to get angry and upset. He now wished he had throttled Albert in the corridor where no one could have seen him.

Trying hard to appear unperturbed by the old man, Edward continued to eat the bread and cheese and he sat staring at him as he ate. Sarah tried to calm Albert down and asked him to excuse Edward's behaviour.

"He's grieving." she offered, "Let him be."

"The lad has no respect." said Mrs Holland, as her attention turned back to the vegetables, "Spoilt, that's what he is. We thought he would be."

Edward glanced over at her before staring back at Albert. They had obviously been talking about him together before he arrived and had worked themselves up.

The old man was stood leering at him across the table, his face contorted with anger. He looked adamant to prove to himself that whatever they had assumed about him earlier was true.

"You haven't given him a chance, Anne," added Sarah, "Albert, please."

The old man's grimace slowly dropped as he looked at Sarah.

"I won't have him speak to me like that again," he said, sternly, "I demand respect."

Edward finished off the stale bread and pushed the tray of cheese aside.

"I know you don't want me here," he said, looking over at Mrs Holland and then back at the old man, "I don't want me here either. I only found out an hour ago that Sarah was my new guardian and that I'll be working as a gardener, or something."

He stood up still clutching the cheese knife. "As far as I'm concerned I have nothing else to lose. I don't care if I get kicked out of here and sent back to the kid's home, I hope I do, so go ahead, have me flogged, I don't give a shit, but don't think for one second that it will earn you any respect from me."

Sarah grabbed his arm in an attempt to calm him down and retrieve the knife.

"Let me show you your room?" she said reassuringly, "We can start afresh tomorrow when everyone's calmed down."

She had begun to prise the knife from his fingers just as the chauffeur entered the kitchen from outside and all eyes turned to him. The man could see that something untoward was afoot and he took off his cap as he closed the door. He stood next to Albert and asked what was going on. He had already spied the weapon the boy was clutching.

Connor was a big man and afraid of no one. Edward's father had spoken about him on several occasions with tales of his strength and fighting prowess. His face definitely painted a picture of his previous battles from his flattened boxers nose to the long scar across his jaw. He wasn't someone a thirteen year old boy could trifle with.

"Drop the knife Edward," he said, placing his cap on the table, "What would your father think?"

Sighing heavily, Edward relinquished the cheese knife and Sarah got to her feet. She looked a little shaken but managed a meek smile.

"I'll go and show Edward his room," she said, looking at Albert with pleading eyes. "Is that ok, Albert?" she asked.

The old man said nothing. He looked unsure of himself and was still focussed on the knife.

"I wasn't planning to use it," Edward said, "I didn't even know I was holding it until Sarah grabbed my hand,"

Albert turned to leave the kitchen. "Just get him out of my sight," he growled, and left the room.

Mrs Holland looked flabbergasted that Albert had not reprimanded the boy for his impudence but said nothing as she watched him leave.

"Not the best start, ay lad?" said Connor with a wry smile.

"Everybody hates me," said Edward, picking up his bag. "I wish I was back at the home."

"That's not true, Edward, I don't hate you. I'm glad you're here," Sarah said softly, "Let's get you settled in. Things will look better tomorrow."

Connor agreed with her and asked if he could accompany them to his room.

4

Edward and Connor followed Sarah across a paved courtyard to a converted barn opposite the kitchen. It was a long stone building with dormer windows and two separate entrance doors.

A tall stone wall, that spanned the length of the yard and topped with slabs, linked the barn to the manor house. A series of stables with large metal gates at either end completed the enclosure.

The gates at the bottom end that were linked to the barn gave access to the grounds beyond the manor house. Edward could see a man in the distance, through the bars in the gates, lopping the lower branches off a tree. He assumed it was the man he would be working under but could not recall being told his name.

"I recognised you from a photograph your father showed me." Connor informed Edward as they walked, "He loved you very much."

Edward felt a lump forming in his throat as he heard of his father's love for him. Gareth had been a good father, strong and caring but had never once told Edward that he loved him. It was strangely upsetting to hear, especially said out loud.

"I recognised you from a photo too," Edward replied. He could feel his voice quivering a little as he struggled to keep a brave face. "One where you're in the army."

Connor chuckled. "Ah, yes, the army. I could tell you a few tales about your father and I," he said, "It's a shame we lost touch because we were good friends."

"Lost touch?"

"Yes, I hadn't seen him since leaving back in 46 but I bumped into him about six months ago. It was your dad who got me this job."

Edward desperately needed someone he could trust, someone who's loyalties were not with the Carter family or anyone associated with them. Learning that Connor had only been working here for a few months meant that there was a chance he could be trusted.

However, Edward was wary. The man had been friends with his father once, and did seem to be a kind and decent man but, could he tell him of his suspicion about his dad's death?

Sarah led them into the barn and on entering they found themselves in a small lobby with a door either side and a flight of stairs directly in front. There was barely enough room for them all and Edward was forced to mount the first step so that Sarah could close the door. She quickly showed Edward the ground floor rooms.

The room on the left of the stairs as they entered was a kitchen diner shared by the staff and there was a small bathroom at the far end. The room on the right was a lounge situated in the centre of the building. There were two sofa's with a coffee table between them, a radio set near the window and there was another door on the opposite side that led to another lobby with a second staircase with another room beyond that.

After explaining the layout Miss Roberts led them both up the flight of creaky stairs, to a small square landing with two doors.

"This is your room Edward," she said, entering the room above the kitchen diner. "and that's mine opposite."

Edward followed her in and made his way over to the single bed that was positioned between two dormer windows. He flopped his bag to the floor and peered out onto the courtyard below.

The dormers gave a good view of the main house. There was a single storey extension that spanned the entire length of the building. Edward could tell that the kitchen and the courtyard wall were built at the same time as the manor but the rest looked fairly new and there were several large roof lanterns and patio doors. He eyed the long narrow roof windows along the rear wall of the manor that had lit his way to the kitchen earlier.

The first floor windows were all higher than his, including double doors with Juliet Balconies at either end of the property. There were also a couple of large wooden Louvre screens positioned almost central to the manor and set below sill level.

Edward wondered if anyone was watching him from one of the many windows before flopping himself onto the bed. Connor was stood looking out at the rear grounds of the manor through a sloping roof window on the opposite side of the room.

Smiling, Sarah asked if he liked his room and Edward nodded as he gave it the once over. He spotted several boxes of his belongings on the floor at the foot of the bed but let them be for now.

Curious, Edward asked Connor if he also had a room in the barn.

"Oh, I don't stay here," he answered, stepping across to the dormer opposite. He looked out for a few moments before continuing, "I have a place in town about ten minutes drive away."

"But, what if Mr Carter needs you?"

"Don't worry, he's thought of that," was the reply, "he's had one of those damn telephones fitted in my flat."

He sat next to Edward on his bed and looked over at Sarah.

"Look," he said, putting his arm across Edward's shoulders, "We know that your life has been turned upside down but, it's nobodies fault and you mustn't let the likes of Albert get to you."

Edward knew that Connor was referring to him holding the knife in the kitchen earlier and could not tell whether he was concerned for him or the old man. He felt that the incident was being blown out of all proportion but didn't comment, instead he simply nodded in agreement.

It was Sarah who reminded Connor that he hadn't realised he was even holding the knife and all had been forgotten.

"By you perhaps," said Connor standing up, "but he needs that old man on his side if he wants to live here hassle free and you can guarantee he won't forget."

"Then, he'll apologise to him tomorrow," offered Sarah, smiling at her young charge, "Won't you, Edward?"

Again, Edward made no comment and simply nodded in agreement. He hated the idea of grovelling but, if it made the matter go away, then so be it.

"Good," said Connor, with a sigh of relief, "it's for the best. You don't have to like him, just keep him sweet."

Sarah glanced at her watch, "I have to go, cook will be ripping her hair out," she remarked, "I'll bring you something to eat later Edward, ok?"

The lad gave a thankful smile and she left his bedroom and made her way down the creaking stairs and out through the front door.

"She's a good woman, Edward." said Connor as he watched her crossing the courtyard towards the kitchen. "She's genuine, you now?"

He looked at Edward as he spoke but the boy had lifted one of the boxes on to the bed and was prizing it open. "I feel you can trust her," he added.

Edward glanced at him briefly at the word trust. He did like Sarah but, as far as trusting her went, he hadn't had enough time to make up his mind. He felt that if she had to choose between him and her job at the moment the job would win. That could change in the future but, for now, he was sure that her loyalty was with the Carter's, or at the very least, with Albert.

"Don't you think so?" asked Connor, turning away from the dormer.

Edward shrugged his shoulders as he rummaged through the box.

"I don't know yet," he replied, "I'm not exactly among friends here."

Connor chuckled and ruffled Edward's hair playfully with his big bruiser fingers.

"You'll soon settle in and find your feet," he said, "besides, you already have two friends in me and Sarah."

"Can you be trusted?" Edward asked bluntly, reaching for another box.

Connor thought for a moment before replying. He knew the boy was having trust issues and that he must be feeling alone and vulnerable.

"Of course I can be trusted." he replied, "Your father had my back in the army and now I have yours."

"But, what about your loyalty to Mr Carter?" Edward searched.

"Mr Carter's a good man, and he's my boss, but any loyalty I have for him is purely a working one, believe me. You ,on the other hand, are more personal because I feel we have history, you know what I mean?"

Edward nodded. Could this man truly be

trusted? He still had reservations on confiding in him but he had to know what Connor knew, or had possibly overheard, about what happened to his dad. It was a leap of faith.

"Do you believe DaSilva's story about how my dad was killed?" he asked, looking into Connor's eyes.

It was beginning to get dark outside and Connor's face was cast in shadow. He looked back at Edward for a moment with an expression of mild surprise at being asked such a question.

"I can see that you don't," he said as he thought about his own feelings towards it. Again, he looked down into the courtyard. "I guess I haven't really questioned it," he confessed.

"But, his story doesn't make sense," explained Edward, "If there were two men coming after me I wouldn't just shoot one of them and then kill myself, would you?"

Connor shrugged his shoulders as he gave it some thought. "Who knows how anyone would react in that situation?"

"Well, I for one would have either killed them both or none at all. Why bother shooting in the first place if you had no intention of finishing the job? It just doesn't make sense."

"So, what do you think happened?"

Edward gave a long sigh as he decided whether or not to tell him what he really thought had happened. He knew once it was said out loud there would be no taking it back. However, he felt he had nothing to loose.

"I think DaSilva killed them both and made it look like Charles Walker shot my dad and then himself."

"But, why would DaSilva kill your dad, what possible reason would he have to do it?"

"I don't know, there's just something telling me it was him."

Connor looked down at the boy, who's big brown eyes were staring right back at him. They were pleading with him to believe his accusation.

"You're just tired and upset and looking for someone to blame."

"No! I'm not. I know it was him and I'm going to prove it,"

"Look, DaSilva was ruled out as a suspect during the investigation, the only fingerprints found on the gun were those of Walker's."

"It was him." snapped Edward.

Shaking his head, Connor made his way to the door and looked back at Edward as he opened it. "I admit the guy is a bit unsociable but, a murderer. You're jumping to conclusions and if I were you I wouldn't mention this to anyone else."

"But!"

"Drop it Edward!"

Not wanting to hear anymore, Connor left the room. Edward listened for the middle steps to creak followed by the sound of the door closing. He jumped to his feet and looked down on the man as he walked towards the kitchen.

Edward was already rueing his decision to tell him his theory. He point blank refused to even accept that DaSilva could be lying and now thinks Edward is grief stricken and delusional.

With hindsight, there was no point telling him anything at all because there is nothing he could do to help him anyway. It would probably make it harder for him to find out the truth if someone else was involved and there was always the chance that they would talk and warn the enemy.

"Keep your mouth shut," Edward whispered, as Connor disappeared into the kitchen.

He felt he had betrayed himself and swore then and there to never let it happen again. Connor was now more likely to keep an eye on him, ask of his whereabouts when absent and more likely to question his movements or plans. Edward had made a mistake and had learned the hard way. Trust no one.

The last rays of sunshine were diminishing up the wall of the courtyard and his bedroom was beginning to get quite dark. Edward rested his elbows on the narrow window sill of one of the dormers as he scanned the manor house opposite.

His eyes were drawn to movement coming from the ground floor patio doors but could not quite see what it was. A curtain was swaying gently as if someone had just moved it but his view was obscured by the wall connecting the barn with the main house.

Standing on his tiptoes, he strained his neck

to see more clearly. A girl, around five or six was sitting on the floor and looking into the garden as she poked at the glass. Her mouth was moving and she appeared to be singing to herself.

It was the first time he had seen little Marie. His father had told him about her, of how spoilt she was and of how bad tempered she could get. It was hard for him to imagine her that way as she played so innocently.

Just then, through his peripheral vision, movement elsewhere caught his attention. It had come from the doors behind the Juliet balcony almost opposite his room. He scanned them and, at first, could see nothing untoward but, as he was about to gaze back at Marie, he saw it again.

It was a figure. Someone was trying to conceal themselves behind a curtain but their shoulder and part of their face were visible. He recognised the light grey suit and knew instantly who it was. DaSilva was spying on him.

Edward stepped away from the window and into the shadows as a cold chill ran through him. He struggled to remain calm as he stood staring at the partial figure that was looking back at him.

DaSilva clearly had it in for Edward but the boy knew that this was a time for rational thinking and not hysterics. As his heart beat through his ribs he tried to assess the situation.

The fact that the man was spying at all bolstered his suspicions about him, and his pathetic story, but Edward now realised he had been a fool. The look he had given the man at the funeral had made him curious, set alarm bells ringing, and he was now on to him.

Edward had betrayed himself twice in one day and he clenched his teeth in anger and frustration. He had a lot to learn. The enemy was now aware of his interest in him and would be more wary and vigilant.

DaSilva's actions were speaking louder than words to Edward. If he had nothing to hide then why go out of his way to spy? This was clearly a man with a guilty conscience and something to hide who felt that Edward was a threat.

The boy was determined to show he was not afraid and, with hindsight, did something else that was foolish. He stepped back to the window and waved. The curtain swayed gently as the figure disappeared.

5

The next morning Edward awoke to the sound of muffled voices in the kitchen below him. He stretched and yawned as he looked around his room. The late winter sun was shining through the sloping roof window, casting a trapezoid of light on the door, and the sky looked blue and cloudless.

The remnants of last nights supper, a lamb sandwich that Sarah had bought him, littered his bed. He brushed the bread crumbs to the floor before sitting up and pulling on his socks. It was Saturday and he had the day to himself, unlike the rest of the staff who worked in the big house.

His eyes were drawn to a photograph of his mother that lay amongst others near the boxes on the floor. He had emptied them out last night but had been too tired to go through them. He bent forward and picked it up.

Her passing was as raw now as it was seven years ago and there were still elements of her death that puzzled him.

He had been told that the cause of the fire that killed her was most likely a cigarette. It had started in one of the bedrooms but accelerants were found in the house and fowl play could not be ruled out.

Both bodies had almost been incinerated in the heat of the flames and could only be identified by a few remaining teeth. His mother's wedding ring was also found in the ashes which his father indentified by the inscription on the inside.

There were many questions without answers and he had to stop dwelling on the past. Edward was now an orphan and perhaps Albert and Mrs Holland were right. The sooner he accepted his situation the easier it would be. The life he knew was gone and the only person he could truly trust was himself. He had to man up and face whatever was in store for him head on and alone.

The smell of fried bacon wafting into his room was making him hungry and he quickly got dressed and made his way down stairs. As he neared the kitchen door unfamiliar voices could be heard but the creaking steps betrayed him and the talking stopped.

He stood outside the door apprehensively and listened for a moment before summoning up the courage to open it. Edward was not normally shy but for some reason he was feeling that way now. He had to remind himself of his earlier promise, to man up.

He opened the door and stepped into the kitchen. Sarah was standing over a small stove in the far corner cooking breakfast for three strangers who were all sat around a table. Their eyes turned to him as he entered.

A man in his late fifties, his shirt sleeves rolled up passed his elbows, was looking up at him. Sat next to him was a younger man with ginger hair, freckles and a moustache and a girl, dressed as a maid, sat opposite him. She was not much older than Edward and was pleasantly attractive. She had twisted herself round on the bench to see him.

Feeling a little uncomfortable, Edward greeted them all with a smile and a couple of awkward nods of his head. Coming to his rescue Sarah introduced him to them and asked him to take a seat. stepping over the long bench he slid in beside the maid.

The older man reached across the table. He had narrow shoulders and a long thin face with yellowing teeth.

"Jim Dawson," he said, as they shook hands, "Grounds man."

"Nice to meet you sir,"

Jim chuckled at the boy's politeness, "Dawson will do ."

"I'm Stefan," said the other man in a Scottish accent, also offering to shake hands, "er, animal welfare,"

Again, Dawson chuckled, "He means Stable boy."

The man gave Dawson a stern look before chuckling himself.

"Well, ok yes," he confessed, looking back at Edward, "It's just the title 'Stable boy'. I'm twenty nine for god's sake."

"And I'm Lisa." said the girl interrupting.

Edward looked at the maid. She had big blue eyes and perfect skin. Her brunette hair was tucked beneath a white bonnet and there were tufts of it hanging down across the forehead. Edward was instantly smitten.

"Junior house maid." she added.

Edward felt his cheeks redden as he blushed which made Lisa smile as she began eating her bacon and eggs. Before long everyone was sat eating and engrossed in casual conversation, during which, Edward learned of everyone's role in the manor house.

The house staff worked seven days a week with Sunday afternoons off. The ancillary staff such as the grounds man, stable hand and chauffeur had a five day week but must be on hand whenever needed. There were also a few part time staff who came in two or three times a week for laundry duties and so on.

Everyone sat there at the table lived in the converted barn. Albert and his wife, Mildred, who was the head maid, lived in the stately home along with Mrs Holland, the head cook and recent widow.

They had just started to ask Edward questions when they were interrupted by a bell ringing on the wall above the bathroom door. It was on a board with several others and was swaying on a spring bracket. Each bell had the name of a room below it.

Wiping her mouth on a napkin, Lisa got to her feet. It was almost 7:30 and she had been summoned for duty.

"It's nice to meet you Edward," she said with a beautiful smile, "I hope we'll be friends."

"Yes," he spluttered, struggling to swallow the last of the toast, "same to you, and me too."

The maid left and Sarah began collecting the breakfast plates. Edward slid his across the table for her.

"Be careful what you say to that one," said Dawson, finishing off his mug of tea, "unless you want all and sundry to know your business."

"She probably feels it's her duty to blab," added Stefan, "being Albert's granddaughter and all."

"Granddaughter?" exclaimed Edward, "she never said."

Albert had obviously told her all about him, he must have, but she never mentioned it once, no one did. Perhaps she wanted to make up her own mind about him but still, it was odd not to mention it. After all, everyone else had made a song and dance about him and the knife and it was difficult to think that the old man had kept it to himself.

"Is Albert the butler or something?" he enquired.

"Head of staff," Dawson informed him.

As she washed the dishes Sarah explained that when the Carter's bought the property ten years ago it came with most of the staff here today, with the exception of Stefan and Lisa.

Albert was the butler for the previous owners but Mr Carter wanted to tone down the formality and pomp and made a few changes. He wanted the manor house to be more homely and relaxed the rules a little making Albert the head of staff and removing several duties like answering the telephone, sorting out his clothes or dressing him and so on.

"Mr Carter's a good man," added Dawson, "firm but fair."

Edward silently disagreed.

6

Dawson offered to show Edward around the estate to help familiarise him with the layout of the site ready for work on Monday. They left Sarah and Stefan in the kitchen and made their way across the courtyard.

Edward followed the tall, sinewy, man through the gate attached to the side of the manor house and was led around to the front of the building. There was a chill in the morning air but the sun was just warm enough to take the edge off it. Edward buttoned his jacket.

Most of the ground was still sodden from yesterdays showers and they kept to the gravel and slabs. Dawson pointed out several maintenance jobs to be done as they walked. A section of wall that formed the flower beds had collapsed, some perimeter slabs needed re-laying and he mentioned the garage roof was in disrepair.

"We're not just gardeners," he told Edward, "We're caretakers too and there's plenty of work to be done on and inside the house itself."

Edward looked around. The site was large and Dawson had done well to keep it as clean and tidy as he had.

"How do you decide what needs doing first?" he asked, showing interest, "the place is huge."

"Oh, I usually get the garden aspect out of the

way first, cutting the main lawn, pruning bushes, bedding plants and such like," he explained, "and then I go round fixing things I've spotted, like that damn wall."

Edward chuckled.

"And now you have me to help you," he said, actually feeling a little better about having to stay here and work for his keep. Jim seemed to be a considerate sort of man but Edward decided to reserve judgement until he had worked for him a while. After all, anyone would seem nice during a lazy Saturday morning stroll.

They made their way across the front of the building, passed the stone portico with its stepped plinth and on to the other side. There was a double detached garage set back a few metres and Dawson showed him the hole in the roof as they walked by it.

The passage between the garage and the house led into the rear garden via a rickety gate. The huge lawn was enclosed by a privet and there was a tall trellis archway in the centre with gates. Keeping to the perimeter slabs near the house they made their way across to the patio area.

"When Spring comes the lawn will need cutting once a fortnight, weather permitted," explained Dawson, "and the hedge trimmed both sides."

The man's words were not for information purposes but were instructions and Edward scanned the garden. It was no small task, especially if the person expected to do it had never even tidied up his own room. It was a time for him to reflect on how good he had had it before losing everything.

"The cuttings go in the composter behind the stables." added Dawson, "but, with winter coming, it won't need doing for a while yet."

As they stood on the patio, Edward glanced back into the house. Beyond his own reflection he could see a huge room with lavish furnishings and large paintings on the walls. Large decorative pots on stands were dotted around the perimeter and a snooker table took centre stage.

There were several pieces of paper on the carpet near the doors and Edward stepped in for a closer look. They were drawings of the garden that Marie had done in coloured crayon. She must have been doing them yesterday when he had spied her from his room. He smiled as he remembered his own box of crayons he had when he was her age.

He would sit for hours colouring in pictures from a thick book with his mom on the sitting room floor. She showed him how to colour more evenly and stay within the lines and how to fill the pictures with lines and dots instead. How he wished he could go back in time and spend another day with her.

"Pay attention Edward," said Dawson, walking away, "we haven't finished yet."

Edward caught up with the ground's man who then gave him a piece of advice which, at first, took the lad by surprise.

"It's rude to glare through windows, son," he said, sternly, "don't do it again."

Although he had not been glaring in on anyone Edward could see his point and said nothing. He had to learn how to conduct himself around the manor and the occasional mild reprimand had to be accepted without protest. He decided to let the matter go.

They were now on the other side of the courtyard wall that was topped with slabs. It was adjoined to the manor house but ran along the side of the barn and continued on passed it for the length of the garden. It gradually diminished in stages until it was the same height as the privet.

Edward followed Dawson through a gate in the wall that led to a cobbled area behind the barn. There were several empty pig sties and a couple of outhouses. One was used to store building materials like sand and cement and the other, larger and padlocked, was for the gardening tools.

Dawson removed the padlock and showed Edward some of the tools he would need for the lawn and put them to one side for him. He pointed at a green lawn mower with an engine and grass box.

"Petrol," he said, pointing down at it, "Don't worry, I'll show you how to use it before letting you loose."

Edward, who was praying it would rain for the next few months , smiled and tried to look enthusiastic. Dawson handed Edward the key before closing the door and replacing the padlock.

"That's your copy," he said proudly, as if he were handing Edward a gift, "Had it done my self so don't lose it."

Edward thanked him and stuffed the key into his jacket pocket. Although he had been listening to Jim as they made their way around the estate his thoughts had been elsewhere. He could not shake the image of DaSilva spying on him.

It had unnerved him more than he would care to admit and had spent half the night going over it in his head. He deeply regretted waving at him and knew it had made matters worse. He hated himself for being so hot headed.

Trying to appear as if he were making casual conversation as they walked he asked Dawson if Mrs Carter was Spanish. He really wanted to know more about DaSilva but did not want to flag up any more suspicion and decided for a less direct route.

"Only, she speaks with an accent," he added.

The tall scrawny man led Edward back into the courtyard via the metal gate.

"She's Portuguese," he informed him as he opened it, "but she's lived in Britain most of her life. Her family owns the shipping part of the Carter business."

"Oh, and DaSilva?"

"He's her cousin."

Edward swung the gate closed for Dawson and slid the catch across.

"I don't think he likes me," he said nonchalantly.

"I wouldn't take it personal lad, he's not exactly the friendly type."

Edward sensed an air of disdain in his voice and could tell that Dawson had mixed feelings towards him.

"Do you like him?" he pried, as they made their way into the stables.

Instead of answering him, Dawson looked at Edward and shook his head but then shushed him before they entered. It was clear that he did not want his feelings to be heard.

Stefan was in the stable grooming a small brown pony and he greeted them both as they entered. Edward could only assume that it was Stefan the shush was aimed at and he made a mental note to be wary of him in the future.

"Mrs Carter's taking the lassie riding," explained Stefan, as he continued to brush the pony's back, "I've got ten minutes to get them both ready."

Behind him was a big black horse eating from a wooden trough and Dawson made his way right to it. The aroma of straw and urine was quite strong and it took a little getting used to.

"Come and meet Storm," he said slapping the horse's back.

Storm stopped eating and stepped back a few paces while nodding its head and Dawson grabbed the reigns. "She's a beauty," he added as Edward approached cautiously.

The lad had to agree, Storm was a magnificent specimen with her fine coat and perfect muscle definition. She looked both powerful and elegant at the same time, the epitome of fitness.

Dawson began grooming her and he asked Edward to bring him her saddle that was on a bracket on the wall opposite. It was a little heavier than he had expected and almost dropped it to the ground.

With experienced hands, Dawson threw the saddle onto her back and fastened the straps. Stefan had done the same to the pony and together they led the animals out into the courtyard.

Sophia was looking through the kitchen window as they emerged from the stable and Edward turned away the moment he had spotted her. He found the sound of the hooves on the courtyard paving slabs quite pleasant and concentrated on that.

Within seconds Marie came running over followed closely by her mother. They were wearing matching equestrian outfits, from their tight jodhpurs, boots and jackets, to their crops and riding helmets.

Stefan helped young Marie up onto her saddle but Sophia expertly mounted Storm herself and instantly bought her to attention. Although Edward disliked the woman she had impressed him. Not only by her confidence with the horse but by the way she looked in her outfit.

She was the kind of woman that dressed to impress no matter what the occasion and she had not let herself down today. With less make-up than usual she looked quite attractive and he caught Stefan ogling her.

Marie began staring at Edward, it was the first time she had seen him and was not used to strangers. At first he smiled at her but once he realised it was not a friendly look he turned away. She was not an ugly child but her permanent frown did her no favours.

Sophia had done her best not to look at Edward and instructed Dawson to open the gate before trotting out of the courtyard followed by Marie, who stuck her tongue out at Edward as she passed him..

"Pay no attention Ed," said Stefan, as they disappeared out of sight, "she's just a child."

Edward huffed and smiled wryly. "A spoilt brat more like," he said.

The tour of the estate was over and he followed Dawson back into the kitchen of the converted barn. The ground's man lit the stove and filled the kettle and entertained Edward with a tale or two from his past as they waited for it to boil.

"Now that you've met everyone what do you think?" he asked, filling the teapot with water.

Edward shrugged his shoulders as he gave a few approving nods of his head. He still had mixed feelings about being there and was unsure what to say.

"It's ok I suppose," he replied, unenthusiastically, " just wish I'd been told that I'd be living here sooner that's all."

"Sooner? We all knew you were coming three or four days ago."

"I was told yesterday at the funeral."

Dawson shook his head disapprovingly as he swilled the teapot around to make the brew richer.

"No wonder you're so miserable."

He sat himself down at the table opposite the boy.

"Don't worry lad, I treat as I find and I feel you and I will get on like a house on fire," he said, sliding a cup across the table for Edward.

A poor choice of words, being that his mother died in one, but Edward did not react. He knew that the man had meant well so instead he simply smiled and nodded in thanks. It was reassuring to know that he was on his side and would be treating him fairly.

"Being the gardener I didn't really know your dad that well," confessed Dawson, "but we waved and nodded at each other quite a lot in passing. He seemed like a good man."

As they supped Edward told him more about Gareth Kane. About his sense of humour, his fighting skills and strength but was interrupted by Albert entering the kitchen before he could tell him anything about his mother.

"Mr Carter would like to see you, Edward," he

said, giving a nod of welcome to Dawson as he stood by the door ready to escort Edward out.

7

Edward followed Albert out of the kitchen and across the yard. The old man still seemed offish with him and was quiet. It was time for that apology Sarah had promised.

"I'm sorry for my behaviour yesterday," he said, as they entered the kitchen, "I was upset."

Mrs Holland was kneading dough on the large table as they entered but Sarah was nowhere to be seen. The old woman glanced at them as they walked by but said nothing as she carried on with her task.

Edward thought that his apology had fallen on deaf ears but as soon as they were in the corridor the old man responded.

"I accept your apology, Edward," he said, glancing back at him briefly, "and we'll say no more about it."

Edward thanked him and agreed. He did feel that it was he who deserved the apology but was just glad the matter had finally been forgotten.

He followed the head of staff across the large entrance hall and he took in as much as he could as they walked. The sweeping central staircase was the focal point of the room with its ornate balustrade, gaping atrium and crystal chandelier that hung from the first floor ceiling.

Being at the heart of the building the hall had

a symmetrical layout and the right side of the staircase was a perfect mirror image of the left, identically positioned doors at either side of the hall and even a corridor either side of the stairs.

They made their way into a huge dining room via a tall panelled door. A long rectangle table, draped in cloth and with twelve chairs around it, was positioned in the centre and Edward followed Albert around it and through a pair of double doors.

The walls of the next room were hidden behind fitted bookcases that were filled with books of all sizes and Edward was awestruck as he looked around. A glass cabinet to his right, that housed a row of shotguns and rifles was one of only two gaps in the rows of bookcases, the other was a door that must have led to the rear flat roof extension.

Mr Carter was sat at a large desk on the far wall as they entered and was talking to DaSilva who was sat with his back to them. Edward's heart sank a little as he spotted the loathsome man and Albert ushered him along before leaving him alone and closing the door.

"Ah! Edward," exclaimed Mr Carter, cutting DaSilva off in mid sentence as the boy approached, "Just want to keep you informed, is all."

He slid a sheet of paper across the desk for him as he neared and Edward picked it up. Already he could feel DaSilva's eyes burning into him. It was some sort of official document with a lot of small writing on both sides and a space for a signature at the bottom.

"What is it?" he enquired, having no desire to read it.

"It's an update from my solicitor about your father's affairs."

"Affairs?"

"Yes, you know? Money you will inherit and such."

Edward looked confused and Mr Carter felt obliged to explain further about the procedures of probate and the transferring of funds to an account in Edwards name.

"It's not that much really because Gareth was renting the house you lived in so it only leaves his Jag and the money left in the bank, minus any debts he has of course."

Edward had not given his inheritance a single thought but the mere mention of the red Jaguar bought fond memories flooding back. His dad had taken him on trips around the country in it, they had been fishing in it and he had even driven it once. Only the once mind due to him nearly crashing it into a tree.

"What's going to happen to the car?" he asked, glancing back at the document to see if it had been itemised.

"Well, Armando has made an offer to buy it."

"Armando?"

Mr Carter gestured towards DaSilva and Edward cottoned on immediately. A wave of mixed feelings rushed through him in an instant, anger, hatred, betrayal, all unpleasant and all aimed at DaSilva.

"Buy it from who, exactly?" he enquired, trying hard to remain calm. He could feel his demons welling up. Although he had only just been reminded of the car's existence he loathed the idea of DaSilva owning it and would do anything to stop it.

"You, I suppose."

Edward looked down at DaSilva and their eyes locked.

"I'm sorry, but it's not for sale," he said, holding back a scowl.

Armando DaSilva glared back at him with hatred in his eyes. He looked as though he wanted to rip Edward's throat out as he clenched his teeth in suppressed anger and forcing his jaw muscles to bulge. He did not react but it was obvious he was trying hard to appear unfazed.

"Een general or just to me?" he sneered, still clenching his teeth.

He spoke with the same accent as Sophia but his was broader and more pronounced. Edward felt his heart racing in his chest. He knew he had enraged a man capable of murder and felt as though he had just opened the lions cage and was waiting to be mauled.

Edward had to admit that he felt a little afraid of DaSilva who now reminded him of a gangster, a mafia hit man if you will. In his smart suit, black greased back hair, olive skin and dark eyes. He was a sly, seedy looking character that emanated an air of menace. Edward had to chose his next words carefully.

"In general, of course" he replied, eventually, "It's the only thing I have left to remind me of him."

Armando looked at Edward with utter contempt for a moment before turning to Mr Carter. He shook his head and pursed his lips to show his disappointment and his boss felt compelled to comment on the issue.

"It makes no sense holding on to it, Edward" said Mr Carter, leaning back in his large leather chair, "It'll be no good by the time you're old enough to drive and there's the storage problem, I mean, where are you going to keep it?"

Edward shrugged. "Where is it now?" he asked, defiantly. He knew he was about to be bullied into giving it up but was adamant to keep it.

"It's at my local depot," Mr Carter replied, "but it's in the way and I need it shifting."

"I could keep it here behind the barn," offered Edward, thinking on his feet, "or in the empty stable,"

Mr Carter shook his head. "Sophia won't allow anything to upset her precious horse, what with the noise and fumes, she'd see red. No. It has to go Edward."

Edward glanced at DaSilva, "So, where would he keep it?"

"Here of course, but he would use it on a regular basis and not just leave it rotting on my property."

Just then they were interrupted by Connor entering the room who reminded Mr Carter of an appointment he was due to attend. William Carter looked at his watch, stood up and slid on his suit jacket.

Connor looked a little flustered, as if he had been waiting a while for Mr Carter to arrive and had been forced to come and get him. Edward remembered that weekends were normally his own and he was obviously a little put out. They never even made eye contact and he had disappeared within seconds.

"Take the offer, Edward," said Mr Carter, collecting a few things from one of the desk drawers, "It'll be in good hands and it's money in the bank."

And with that, he left, leaving Edward alone with Armando DaSilva who waited for the door to close before standing up.

They stared at each other for a moment, both sizing up their opponent. It was only for a moment or two but Edward sensed he was in danger as the man glared at him without flinching. Edward was first to look away and DaSilva smiled smugly.

"Have you got a problem weeth me?," he asked, stepping closer, "Have I offended you een some way."

Edward knew that the Portuguese hit man was not referring to the sale of the car but what had happened recently between them. He had to keep his wits about him. He had obviously made the guy suspicious of him and he needed to throw him off the scent.

He was beginning to feel trapped and just wanted to leave but his hot headed stubbornness was too strong.

"But, we have nothing to say," said Edward, trying to keep the conversation focussed on the Jag, "The car's not for sale."

In his heart, he knew that his scumbag had killed his dad but could not afford to let on, not yet, not until he had proof and proof enough for revenge. He had promised himself that he would kill DaSilva with his own hands if his assumption turned out to be true.

"I deesagree," said Armando, clenching his teeth again and ignoring the comment about the car, "There ees a tension between us."

The wretch was now just a few feet away. He was taller than Edward, broader and bigger built. There was a faint scar across his left eyebrow and one of his front teeth was chipped. Signs of a violent past perhaps.

"I don't know what you mean," said Edward, tensing up.

DaSilva stepped ever closer until they were almost touching noses. Edward could now smell his fetid breath and feel its warmth of it on his face as he breathed. He stood and stared into the boys eyes for a moment before speaking.

"Then why the dirty look?"

Trying to appear ignorant Edward shrugged his shoulders and did his best to force an expression of bewilderment. "What look?" he said, innocently.

DaSilva smirked and shook his head. He knew that the boy was playing dumb and was unlikely to confess anything with this approach but, he could also see that the boy was afraid and this pleased him. Edward watched the mans ego growing before him as he raised his head and puffed out his chest.

"You know what look" he snarled.

The man was clearly provoking a confrontation, it was as though he wanted Edward to react so that he would have an excuse to thump him. Edward swallowed nervously as he thought of a reply.

"You mean, when I wanted to see how upset everyone was?" Edward queried, "You just happened to be looking at me, that's all."

DaSilva frowned as his eyes narrowed. A glimmer of uncertainty washed across his face and his chest deflated slightly.

"No, you glared at me with hate een your eyes," he remarked.

"I was waiting for a nod or sympathetic smile," Edward retorted, "but all I got was a grimace."

Armando's chest deflated further. The explanation did sound plausible and the man was beginning to question his own actions. Doubt had formed.

"You've made a mistake," added Edward.

"I don't make meestakes," sneered DaSilva, defiantly.

"Jumped to conclusions then," offered the boy.

Edward could tell that the second rate hit man was having doubts and the urge to go further overwhelmed him. The man was almost on the back foot and he just needed a little push, if Edward could keep his nerve.

"I was the one who got the dirty look," he commented, daring to enrage the man further.

DaSilva's eyes widened at the boys remark.

"And the one being spied on last night," he added, courageously.

Armando huffed disdainfully and turned away, knocking Edward back a little with his shoulder as he did so. He meandered over to the window and looked out onto the fountain in the driveway as he remembered skulking behind the curtains.

"I deedn't like the way you looked at me," he said, keeping his eyes fixed outside, "Eet was like you were accusing me of somethin."

Edward's heart was thumping in his ribs. He could not believe that DaSilva had confronted him with so little evidence of him doing anything wrong. He was almost pleased with himself for turning the tables on him so easily but knew the sly foreigner had not finished. He still had to be careful even though he was beginning to feel less afraid.

Armando's break in the conversation had given Edward time to think. He quickly realised that DaSilva could not touch him anyway, not without causing himself problems, and this knowledge helped towards his growing confidence.

"I'd just buried my dad," he said, glancing at the door with the thought of leaving, "How would you look?"

He began to make his way across the room in readiness to leave but DaSilva spotted movement in the glass and turned to face him.

"What ees it you theenk I've done?"

The man was not going to let the issue drop any time soon, no matter how often Edward denied him his confrontation, and it seemed as though he was almost goading Edward in to accusing him of murdering his dad.

Edward stopped in his tracks but did not face DaSilva at first. He thought for a moment before responding.

"You tell me," he replied, "You're the one assuming things." He turned his head slowly and faced the second rate gangster. "What DO I think you've done?" he asked, mockingly.

DaSilva's eyes narrowed, just like they had at the funeral, and he clenched his teeth in anger, flaring his nostrils. The moment of realising the question had backfired was clear to see and he had underestimated the boy's pluck which added to his caged rage.

They glared at each other for a few moments

but this time it was Armando DaSilva who turned away. He had said too much and he knew it. Edward smiled to himself as he left the library.

8

Edward made his way across the dining room and out in the main entrance hall where he soon found himself at the foot of the sweeping staircase.

He looked up at the chandelier and at the imposing atrium with its ornate balustrade and he was suddenly struck with an urge to take a quick look. The stairs split in two at a half landing and swept back round to join the atrium on opposite sides. A large portrait of the Carter family hung on the back wall and two large urns stood guard below it.

He listened for signs of DaSilva following behind and looked around to see if anyone was there before mounting the first step. His heart had only just recovered from his clash with the would be gangster but it was now beginning to beat with mild excitement as he dared himself to take more steps.

He had only planned to go far enough to be able to see onto the first floor but soon found himself on the half landing. His senses were on full alert. The risk of being caught gave the situation an edge that increased the thrill factor and Edward loved it.

With still no sight nor sound of anyone around he ascended the flight of stairs to his right. He felt fairly confident in his belief that, if he were to get caught, it would not amount to much in way of punishment. The adventure was worth the risk of being yelled at or being deprived of a meal or two.

The first floor landing was as big as the entrance hall below it and there were several armchairs with side tables dotted around. The three tall arched windows with stained glass let in light of mixed colours but Edward could not help thinking that it was a terrible waste of space, a vast room for nothing.

Not far from the top step was a window seat that was framed in lavish drapes and with views of the grounds to the rear of the property. Edward stood and gazed through it for a moment. He could see the flat roof of the extension below and the end of the converted barn. He leaned forward for a better look, placing his hands on the seat cushion, so as to be able to see his bedroom dormer.

The walls of the window seat were clad in wooden panelling and were quite deep, at least three feet, and there was a sliding vent on the front wall below the cushion that was almost falling out. Edward bent to push it back in but it came off in his hand, one of the spring clips had broken off.

Kneeling down to replace it he could see that the window seat was hollow and he peered inside. The aperture was big enough for his whole body to squeeze through but only dared poke his head in just enough to see inside.

It was dark and draughty but as his eyes adjusted he was able to see that there was a hidden passageway that appeared to span the length of the manor house behind a false wall.

The sound of a door closing on the ground floor startled him and he quickly replaced the vent and slinked across to the atrium balustrade to peer down the stairs. He saw DaSilva's legs disappearing from view as he made his way outside and Edward breathed a sigh of relief.

He should have taken that as a chance to leave but, instead, crept over to the arched windows and looked down on the Portuguese hit man as he lit a cigarette and began mumbling to himself. He was still angry from his run in with Edward and was going over it in his head.

Now that he had a taste of adventure Edward was reluctant to end it and turned his attention to the corridors that led to the bedrooms. With Mr Carter at a meeting and the spoilt brat out riding with her mother he would not get a better opportunity to explore the place and, without further ado, he hurried across the landing.

The central corridor split the East wing of the building in half and there was a door at the far end of it with a well lit lobby. Like the ground floor the East side of the property was a mirror image of the West and Edward glanced back down the opposite corridor for signs of life.

He could now hear faint voices somewhere in the distance but it was difficult to work out from where they were coming. He pressed on regardless. High on adrenalin he was adamant to fulfil his mission.

Peeking into every room he made his way along the passageway until, eventually, he reached the door at the end that had its own lobby and window seat. Cautiously, he opened the door and entered a huge master bedroom with a large four-poster bed against the far wall.

Edward made directly for the double doors with the Juliet balcony and looked across at his own bedroom almost opposite. This is where Armando had spied on him and he visualised the creep skulking behind the curtains for a moment.

A pinstriped suit lying on the bed confirmed who's room he was in and the smell of cigarettes hung thick in the air. As he made his way over to the front window, Edward noticed several items of interest on a dressing table opposite the four-poster - a gold watch, a pair of gold cufflinks and a silver comb, still smeared in hair grease.

As he looked down at them an idea sprang to mind. Just imagine how annoyed DaSilva would be if they were to be misplaced. It was a foolish thought but one that had caught his imagination.

Edward laughed to himself as he picked up the greasy comb, walked over to the bed, and slid it into the inside breast pocket of the suit jacket. It was when he returned for the other items that he noticed the dressing table drawer was ajar.

He opened it a little further and there, amongst a row of neatly folded ties, was a pair of used silk stockings. It wasn't something Edward felt belonged to a man like Armando so, who's were they?

The voices he had heard earlier were getting closer and he knew he should leave but the discovery had intrigued him. Were the stockings Sophia's? DaSilva could have a girlfriend but somehow, Edward doubted that, and felt that the used tights must belong to Mrs Carter.

He knew he could be jumping to conclusions but his keen mind was telling him that he had just discovered something very important. Were they having an affair?

It could just be wishful thinking, or a desperate need to have something against Armando, but, if Edward was right, this could be just the thing he needed for the man to meet his comeuppance. Mr Carter would kill him for sure.

He peered through the door and down the corridor towards the landing. The voices were so close now that he could hear every word and he was sure one of the bedroom doors were open.

He was right. Within seconds of forming his conclusion Lisa stepped out into the corridor. She was followed by an elderly woman, whom he immediately assumed was Mrs Simpson, Lisa's grandmother and Albert's wife.

They were at the first bedroom from the landing and Edward was going to have to time his exit to perfection. Waiting for them to disappear into the next room he emerged into the lobby, closed the door behind him softly and hid behind the wall opposite. His plan was to wait until they had made their way a little closer, entered another room, before bolting down the corridor as quickly as he could. There was a real risk of being seen but it was either that or be found in DaSilva's room.

Lisa emerged from the bedroom and stood in the corridor with the cleaning trolley as she waited for her grandmother. She was questioning why they had to dust and clean rooms that never get used and was being reminded that it was their job to keep the place looking spotless at all times.

"I've told you before that the surfaces and bed sheets are magnets for dust," explained Mrs Simpson, " and, if we keep on top of it, the task remains an easy one."

She closed one door and opened the next.

"Besides," she added, "we are expecting guests soon and the rooms must look their best."

"Guests?" questioned Lisa, brightening and staying close to her grandmother.

"Yes, well yobs really, but it's Mr Carter's turn to host the Transport Trophy, a fighting competition between several of his competitors."

"That sounds brill," exclaimed Lisa excitedly, "Will I be allowed to watch?"

For a moment the the voices went faint as they moved further in to a room and Edward was forced to peer out into the corridor to listen but, to his utter shock, saw Armando on the landing instead.

The man still looked bemused and was striding

towards him grimacing. He made his way along the corridor quite quickly but was forced to stop suddenly as Lisa pushed the trolley out in front of him.

"Oh! I'm sorry Mr DaSilva," she exclaimed, as the trolley rattled from the collision, "I didn't hear you."

Lisa was an attractive young lady and Armando had already flirted with her on several occasions. His annoyed frown melted away in an instant as he looked into her big blue eyes for a moment in silence.

"Will you be entering the competition, sir?" she enquired, feeling a little uncomfortable from his attention.

Mrs Simpson was quick to intervene and scolded Lisa for being so clumsy and for speaking to a member of the family without being addressed first. DaSilva came to her rescue and said that no harm had been done before referring back to her question.

"Would you like me to enter?" he asked, flirtingly.

Lisa felt her cheeks redden. She was no fool and could read the signs of his growing lust. The man was obviously taken with her and she looked at her grandmother for help.

Mrs Simpson, who was already one step in front, ushered her away into the next room.

"Come now Lisa," she said, "we mustn't keep Mr DaSilva from his business."

The slimy man watched them both disappear and he chuckled to himself as he continued on his way. Within seconds he was at his door but was distracted by a strange noise and turned to face the window seat.

He stepped towards it and looked across at that wretched boy's dormer window before leaning in to see more of the courtyard below. He could now hear the sound of Storm's hooves on the slabs.

9

Edward held his breath as DaSilva stood against the window seat above him. He had managed to prise the vent off and scramble into the void just before the man had reached his room but It had been a close call.

In his haste to escape he had snagged his jacket on the frame of the vent and had just managed to struggle free in time to grab the grille but had attracted his attention struggling to replace it. Sophia's return was a stroke of luck and just the distraction he needed.

He watched Armando disappear into his room before turning his attention to the situation he now found himself in. The enclosed twitten was cold and dusty and he was already covered in clinging cobwebs.

The floor level to the hidden passageway was lower than the main floor and he was almost standing upright below the seat, stooping slightly. He peered down between the walls. The large louvers he had seen from his bedroom window let in some light and as his eyes adjusted more detail became apparent.

Cautiously, he made his way towards the window seat on the landing, the one that had saved his skin. If that vent had not fallen off when it did he wouldn't have known how to evade capture just now.

Every room had its own window seat and he ducked below each one and peered through each vent as he passed them. The thought of climbing out into one of the rooms had crossed his mind but he had no idea where Lisa was and could not risk being caught.

He came across the first wooden louvre in the wall and stopped to investigate. If only he could dislodge it somehow he would be able get onto the roof. From there he could walk along the courtyard wall and make his way down to the hedge at the bottom of the rear garden.

The aperture had a wooden frame bolted to it and the louvre was attached to that by brackets with chunky slot head screws. It was then that Edward remembered the key Dawson had given him earlier. It had a circular flat bow, or thumb grip, and it fitted the slot perfectly.

The screws were harder to turn than he had hoped and was forced to rest his fingers after unscrewing just one of them. At least he knew that, with a little effort, he could get out that way if he was forced to. He put the key and screw into his pocket.

Before he moved on he tried to dislodge one of the slats. He could see that it was slotted into angled grooves at either end and that it should slide out towards him, but it would not budge. Perhaps from outside it could be forced inwards but he hadn't got the strength to pull it.

He gave up as he heard Marie yelling playfully somewhere down in the hall and decided to stick around for a while longer and spy on the occupants of the manor house. He was beginning to feel hungry but the urge to pry prevailed. Cautiously, he made his way through the narrow twitten.

Before long he was peeking through the vent below the landing window seat. Marie had made her way upstairs and was dancing around the armchairs in the spectrum of light from the arched windows.

Armando was quick to make an appearance and he met Sophia as she made her way up the stairs. She remained just out of sight but Edward could still see DaSilva. The man was saying something but he could not hear what because the brat was still singing with an annoying yell.

He pressed his face up against the brass grill but was forced to catch it and pull it back in before it fell away. It clicked into place, just as the other one had, and Armando glanced in his direction for a few seconds. Edward's heart skipped a beat as they glared at each other briefly.

Luckily, Armando's attention was brief and the trio began to walk away towards the opposite corridor. Edward had already assumed that there would be an identical master bedroom in the other wing and, being careful with the vent as he let go of it, he followed them.

Suddenly, as he reached the back of the

staircase, his foot disappeared into the darkness and he toppled forwards frantically flailing his hands blindly for something to grab. To his relief, he felt the cold steel of a wall ladder and managed to save himself from a terrible fall.

There was a gap in the boards of the passage for access from the ground floor and once he had recovered from the shock of almost dying, Edward stepped from the ladder and onto the other side.

He knew he had made a noise loud enough for Armando to hear but was hoping Marie's dreadful singing had drowned it out. He stood motionless for a few seconds as he waited for some kind of a reaction but was relieved when nothing happened.

He made his way along the twitten, swiping cobwebs aside as he went. He ducked beneath the many window seats until he finally reached the other master bedroom. Because there were double doors to this room the vent butted up against the panelling and there was more head room for Edward to stand upright.

"Just stay away from him," he heard Sophia tell DaSilva as he arrived at the vent, "You haven't said anything have you?"

He saw Armando shrug his shoulders as he struggled to answer. Sophia glared at him as she read his guilty persona.

"Well?" she demanded.

"Wee may have had words," he finally admitted, "but, I said notheenk to raise his suspicion."

Mrs Carter sat at her dressing table and stretched out one leg and waved it at DaSilva who immediately prised the riding boot from her ankle, they then did the same with the other leg.

"I theenk he blames me for his father's murder but, that's as far as it goes." he added.

"Are you sure?" she enquired, picking up the boots, "You sure he doesn't suspect anything else?"

Edward frowned. *"Anything else?"* he whispered to himself. What had she meant by that?

Mrs Carter threw fresh clothes on the bed from her wardrobe and began undressing in front Armando. Edward felt that this was not the first time she had done it and DaSilva looked too relaxed for it never to have happened before as he stood watching her.

She slid off her tight jodhpurs and unbuttoned her blouse, she clearly enjoyed being watched, but it was not until Marie was heard racing down the corridor towards them that she told DaSilva to turn around.

Her behaviour had convinced Edward that he had been right about them and that they were having an affair, cousins or not. They were too familiar with each other and their body language betrayed past intimacies.

Her last remark would not leave his mind. It clung there like glue, telling him that there was more to his father's death than he had thought. She was not concerned that Edward might know DaSilva had killed his dad as long as he was unaware of something else, something bigger and more devastating.

As he stood in the darkness watching her undress, Edward remembered the silk stockings that he had taken from DaSilva's room. He put his hand into his jacket pocket and clenched them tightly as a plan for revenge on the murdering bastard materialised.

Marie was now running around the bedroom trailing a silk scarf behind her as she went. Sophia and Armando both watched her for a moment before looking back at each other without smiling. Their expressions were stern and serious. Without another word, DaSilva left the room.

Was Sophia's last remark aimed at Marie? Was she the something else he should be suspicious about? Suddenly, a cog fell into place.

"Was she even Mr Carter's daughter?"

10

The revelation was shocking. If the secret was to come out it would have devastating consequences because Mr Carter would not only kill DaSilva but likely Sophia too. His father had told him once that his boss had a vile temper and that people were afraid to upset him.

He'd had drivers beaten up in the past for even being suspected of pilfering the goods, never mind actually taking anything, just imagine what he would do to them. Finding out that Marie was someone else's child would send him insane, hell, he would probably kill her too.

Edward made his way back through the hidden passage. His mind was racing. He had only been there for a day and had already uncovered a secret so huge he was afraid to say it out load.

He now had a chance of getting revenge on DaSilva but not without tearing a family apart with it. Although he disliked Sophia, and even Marie for that matter, he did not want to see them harmed. There had to be another way.

He reached the gap in the floor with the access ladder bolted to the wall and paused to think. He could either try to remove the screws from the heavy grille to escape, crawl back through the vent on the landing and hope that no one saw him, or go down the ladder to see if there was third option.

Clinging to the metal rungs he slowly descended but, without the light from the large external vents, the ground floor was almost pitch black at first. If it wasn't for the faint light coming from the vents at the base of the false walls at ground floor level he would have carried on down into the murky basement.

As he clung to the ladder he peered into the abyss. A shiver ran up his back as he listened to the sound of dripping water some distance away. The smell of damp brick or rot had filled his nostrils and he could already feel the cold air beginning to penetrate his clothes.

Something was drawing him down into the darkness but the fear of the unknown kept his fingers tight on the rungs of the ladder. If only he bought his dad's flashlight then perhaps he would have ventured further but, without it, the basement was off limits.

The faint clanking sound reached his ears and his heart stopped for a second or two as he trained his eyes towards it. A strange feeling crept over him as he clung there in the darkness, an eerie sense of being watched.

A icy shiver ran through him and he climbed back up several rungs and stepped from the ladder. His eyes were still adjusting to the darkness but he was able to see just enough. He found himself in an enclosed space. He knew that it was blocked off at both ends by the doors to either side of the staircase.

The walls were all brick apart from a central section of wooden panelling directly behind the staircase and Edward, sensing a possible way out, felt the panels for movement. Luckily, and with a sigh of relief, he found that one of them could be slid upwards in its frame. It stood more proud than the others and had obviously been installed for access purposes.

He crouched down and stepped through the aperture and into the space beneath the half landing before gently lowering the panel. Light coming in through several slits on both sides of the cupboard highlighted small access doors and, clambering over boxes and suitcases, he made his way towards one.

He peered out into the entrance hall and listened for movement before emerging from beneath the staircase and squinting in the light. Edward emerged near the kitchen corridor and wondered if anyone else knew about the hidden passageway and the access panel at the back of the cupboard.

He could not believe he had uncovered so much in so little time but could not afford to congratulate himself just yet, he had to get out first without raising suspicion.

He shook the cobwebs from his hair and dusted himself down as he made his way towards the kitchen, a route he already knew well. As he approached the door he could hear Mrs Holland's voice and he paused before opening it as he thought of a reason why he was there.

He decided that a quick exit was called for and the plan was to make directly for the back door and leave before getting roped into conversation.

Sarah had her back to him as he entered but Mrs Holland was looking right at him as she stood at the table thumbing a pastry lid onto a dish. The old crone threw him daggers as she realised who had just entered.

"Does Albert know you're roaming the house?" she barked, startling Sarah into dropping something back into the sink.

She turned around looking alarmed but saw Edward walking towards her. She gave him a warm smile and asked where he had been but her smile soon dropped when she saw how dusty he was.

"With Armando," he replied, opening the kitchen door, "I'll tell you all about it later."

The two women looked at each other in bewilderment as he disappeared from sight.

"He's up to no good if you ask me!" snapped Mrs Holland.

Back in the barn, Edward made himself a cheese sandwich while mulling over what he had just discovered. There had to be a way of using the revelation against DaSilva.

He hated the guy so much that he was tempted to tell Mr Carter as soon as he got back from his meeting but, fearing the consequences for the family, he knew that it was just false bravado.

It was then, as he threw the butter knife angrily into the sink, that another thought occurred him and one that should have materialised sooner. Had his dad found out about Marie and had DaSilva killed him to keep him quiet?

The more he thought about it the more sense it made. His dad had been murdered to keep the secret safe.

"Why else would DaSilva kill him?" he whispered.

11

A short while later, Edward found himself back in his room. He was stood with his head out of the sloping roof window and was looking out across the countryside deep in thought. A cold breeze had chilled his room.

The grounds of the estate bordered a small forest and Edward could see a church spire poking out above the canopy in the distance. He had just begun to wonder how far it was away when he heard the stairs creak.

He looked at the door and knew that someone was standing on the small landing outside his room. The handle was turned slowly and the door opened cautiously, as if the person entering wanted to go unnoticed.

"Hello?" said Edward apprehensively.

Giving up on their sly entrance the door was pushed open and in stepped Lisa. Edward's eyes brightened as he closed the window.

"Lisa," he said, smiling.

He was pleased to see her but she looked serious and his smile dropped.

"What do you want?" he asked.

She closed the door and made her way over to the dormer window.

"We need to talk," she said, scanning the manor house opposite before turning to face him.

"And I want you to be honest with me," she added, expecting a response.

Confused, Edward nodded.

"Were you in the house earlier, because I'm sure I saw you?"

"Yes, I went to see Mr Carter."

"Did you go up stairs?"

Edward forced a bewildered persona and shook his head.

"Are you sure?" she demanded.

"Yes, why?"

Lisa stared at him for a few moments as she tried to see any signs of lying but Edward's innocent act was too convincing. She sighed and sat down on the edge of his bed.

"Mr DaSilva thinks I've taken something from his room." she said, eventually.

"Taken what?"

Lisa gave him daggers. "I don't know cuz I didn't take anything," she snapped.

"Sorry, I meant did he say what?"

Lisa shook her head.

"And he actually accused you?"

"He didn't have to, his angry glare said it all." she snivelled, "He came out of his room and said that he'd been robbed, gave me such a look and forbade me from entering."

Edward sat down beside her. "And you're here hoping to blame me for it instead"?

She looked at him with tearful eyes for a second or two before turning her frown into a smile and chuckling. "I know it sounds bad Edward but, my job is all about trust. Lose that and you're out the door."

"I bet your Nan defended you though, yes?"

Lisa nodded and sniffed back tears. "But I could tell he didn't believe a word she said. We hadn't even got as far as his room, it's ridiculous. Why would I take anything it just doesn't make sense?"

Edward thought for a moment. He wanted so much to tell Lisa that it was he who stole from DaSilva but he didn't want her involved in the reasons why. He also knew it would be wrong of him to let her take the blame for his actions and felt responsible for her being so upset. He had to put it right.

"Then blame me," he said, putting his arm around her.

If he could not tell Mr Carter direct about the secret without getting others hurt in the process then perhaps he could tell DaSilva that he knew about it and get him to back off. It was Lisa's turn to look bewildered.

"You serious?"

"Yes."

"You'd do that for me?"

"Yes."

"But, you'd get in trouble."

Edward shrugged his shoulders. "What's the worst they could do?" he remarked.

Lisa kissed him on the cheek before standing up and straightening her pinafore.

"Thank you Edward you're a real friend but, are you sure?"

"Yes, but only if someone asks you again. Don't just go and drop me in it just like that."

Lisa smiled at him, nodded that she understood, and then left his room. He willed her to look up at him as he watched her make her way towards the kitchen and, to his delight, she did. She even gave him a little wave and one of her gorgeous smiles for good measure.

Although he knew that, because of the age gap between them, she probably thought of him more as a younger brother rather than a potential boyfriend but his feelings for her were pure lust. His pubescent hormones had begun to stir and he wished he was four years older.

He sat on his bed and began to sort through another box of his things and before long his mind strayed from Lisa and onto Marie. To stumble on such a huge secret like that was a chance in a million but, had he jumped to conclusions? He was beginning to doubt himself and question the facts.

He looked at the time on his dad's wrist watch that lay on the bedside table. His nerve was about to be tested big time. Lisa was sure to blab, Albert would see to that, and any time now DaSilva will burst into his room looking for answers.

He was going to accuse the man of, not only sleeping with his cousin, but of fathering her child and killing his dad. His proof. A pair of tights.

12

"Your grandfather's looking for you," said Sarah, as Lisa entered the kitchen, "didn't say what for but he looked annoyed."

Lisa filled a glass with water and leaned against the sink. She knew exactly why he was looking for her and felt awful that she was going to blame Edward, but what else could she do?

The lad was willing to be punished for something he hadn't done on her behalf but, then again, she was just as innocent and could end up losing her job for the same thing. She liked Edward, he was tall, smart and quite good looking for a kid, if only he was a little older.

"You don't look surprised," observed Sarah, sprinkling flour onto the table top, "You trying to avoid him?"

Lisa emptied the glass and wiped her mouth on her sleeve. "He thinks I've done something that I haven't, that's all,"

Sarah enquired into what but Lisa shrugged it off and left the kitchen just as Mrs Holland entered it. They passed each other by and Lisa gave a secret sigh of relief as the cook arched her eyebrows at her accusingly. She knew that if she had stayed a moment longer the old trout would have interrogated her about it.

She was a nosy vindictive woman who thought

it her right to be informed of everyone's business. She thrived on gossip and seemed to enjoy stirring the pot and make matters worse in the process.

It wasn't the first time Lisa had been accused of taking something. A few months earlier, Sophia, had misplaced a set of ear rings her mother had given her and the old trout had pointed the finger at Lisa.

"She was the last one in your room Mrs Carter," she had said, *"You know what girls are like with jewellery. I bet Lisa knows where they are."*

Without any proof her room had been searched leaving it ram shackled only for them to turn up a couple of days later in the back of the limousine. Although she received an apology from all her accusers the old trout had looked almost disappointed that Lisa had been vindicated.

At seventeen she had only been at the house a year and was trying her hardest to fit in and keep her nose clean. Most of her friends back in town were struggling for work and one had even turned to prostitution, although she was unaware that anyone knew.

Lisa was determined to make something of herself. She had dreams of starting her own business one day. Hair and beauty perhaps or a nail salon but she needed money to do it and her parents were in no position to help.

Unknown to everyone in the manor house her father was serving a ten year stretch for manslaughter and her mother was an alcoholic living on money her grand parents sent her.

Without their help Lisa would probably be working the streets too but they had managed to wrangle her a job as maid to keep her away from all the bad influences back home.

She hurriedly made her way through the manor house and was hoping to find her grandmother first, she was always protective of her, but was unfortunate enough to bump into Albert instead on the stairs.

"No need to fret Lisa," he said descending down towards her, "I know it wasn't you." The old man looked pensive as he asked her if she had seen Mr DaSilva.

"No, not since he accused me, why?"

She was relieved she was no longer a suspect but was curious about his persona. There was an urgency about him, a sense of anxious excitement. The sly old fox knew who had been in DaSilva's room or, at least, he suspected someone.

"You know who it was don't you?" she asked.

Albert side stepped around her on the stairs but she grabbed his arm before he had time to pass her by, forcing him to stop.

"Who was it," she enquired.

Her grandfather swished his arm free of her grasp, as if repelling a wasp.

"I'm not at liberty to say just yet," he said, clearly annoyed at being grabbed, "not without further proof."

Lisa followed Albert back down the stairs.

"Do you at least know what's been taken?" she enquired.

"No, but that's not the point," he huffed, "Theft is theft regardless of what is stolen."

He stopped in his tracks and turned to face his granddaughter.

"Return to your duties, Lisa" he said, "I have the matter well in hand."

It was then that she noticed he had something clenched in his fist. He had found something incriminating and Lisa was curious as to what it was. She was about to ask him but was forced to hold her tongue as Mr DaSilva appeared from the dining room.

Albert approached him and held out his open hand.

"Do you recognise this, sir?" he enquired.

Armando, his eyes fixed on Lisa at first, looked down at Albert's hand. He looked puzzled for a moment or two as he eyed a small black button but then snatched it from the old mans palm with lightening speed.

He held it up as he examined it.

"Theese is not mine, where did you find eet?" he asked.

"Outside your room, sir," replied Albert proudly, as if no one else could have found it but him, "not far from your door."

Lisa had edged in far a closer look, she had become aware that Mrs Carter was now looking down on them from the atrium above but did not let on as she eyed the button. She recognised it right away and her heart sank.

Armando had seen her persona change from curiosity to cognizance in the blink of an eye and he stepped towards her, holding the button in her face.

"Who's ees it?" he demanded, aggressively.

Shocked by his sudden movement, Lisa stuttered while answering but it was Albert who Armando heard.

"It's Edward's," he had said, standing between them defensively.

13

Edward had heard the commotion coming from the manor house well before it spilled out into the courtyard. He stood at the dormer window and watched as DaSilva stormed towards the barn, followed by everyone else.

"I'll fucking keel him," he heard DaSilva curse as he barged through the entrance door below.

The boy readied himself for the confrontation as he stood by his bed. He knew that the head-to-head was coming sooner or later but was shocked by how quickly Lisa had given him up. He was also surprised that the loathsome man had bought the whole household with him.

Surely he knew what Edward had taken from his room and now he wanted him to give it back in front of everyone? He was obviously caught up in the heat of the moment and had not thought about the consequences.

The bedroom door burst open and Armando immediately launched himself towards Edward. His father had taught him well and the boy dodged the wild haymaker forcing DaSilva to stumble onto the bed.

However, DaSilva was quick to recover. Using the mattress as a spring board he pounced at the lad and forced him up against the dormer by his throat. Edward had managed to throw a few punches before being slammed up against the wall.

The confrontation had not gone to plan and the man had overpowered him easier than he had imagined. By now the others had begun to fill his room but DaSilva warned them not to interfere. With pure hateful rage in his eyes the man squeezed the boys throat harder and harder.

"Come for your tights!?" croaked Edward, struggling to speak.

DaSilva was in no sane mind to listen to anything the lad had to say and continued with his death grip.

"I'm going to fucking keel you!" he cursed.

Edward fumbled about in his pockets. He was desperately searching for the stockings but was beginning to lose consciousness. Somehow, he managed to locate them and he held them up for all to see. A wave of murmurs spread among the onlookers.

"I know about Marie!" he blarted out, in desperation.

As if awaking from a trance, DaSilva released the boy and grabbed the stockings from him, stuffing them into his own trouser pocket. Edward coughed and spluttered as he gasped for air and Sarah came to his aid, helping him onto his bed.

Sophia was standing in the doorway. She had seen and heard everything and knew that everyone else had too. She could already feel her embarrassment welling up and had to stop DaSilva from making things worse. The situation was still salvageable, she had spotted something in her favour.

"That's enough Armando!" she shouted, anxious for the boy to say no more, "Leave Edward alone!"

Still coughing, Edward looked up at DaSilva. The man was scowling back at him, red faced and breathing heavily. Their eyes locked in a gaze of mutual hatred.

"The mistress has spoken!" sneered Edward, delighting in the double meaning of the word.

DaSilva's eyes narrowed to slits as he clenched his jaw, making the muscles dance. He wanted so much to throttle the boy to death.

"Chop chop!" added Edward.

Sophia was a clever woman and was about to turn the tables on the wretched lad. She forced her way through the group and demanded that DaSilva hand her the stockings. He looked at her questioningly.

"The stockings!" she demanded.

Reluctantly, Armando passed them to her.

She carefully examined them before passing them over to Mrs Simpson.

"You are the one who acquires these for me, are you not?" she said, confidently.

Mildred examined them, thumbing at a small red label, and confirmed that she was the one who collected her under garments from a store in town while visiting her daughter.

"Are they mine?" asked Sophia, glaring at Edward.

"No, Mrs Carter, they're not." she confirmed, "yours have a white label,"

Again, murmurs were heard among the group of witnesses behind her. She stepped towards the boy who was still being comforted by Sarah.

" You are a thief, Edward," she snarled, "and one with an over active imagination."

Edward glared up at her. She had managed to save face and undermined him in one fell swoop but he was too angry to just curl up and surrender. This bitch knew that DaSilva had killed his dad and she had probably ordered it. He was adamant that Marie was the cause.

He stood up to face her directly and Armando reacted. Sophia held out her arm as a signal for him to stay put but he was already at Edward's side with his hands around his neck.

"Armando!" she snapped.

Grimacing, the slimy hit man reluctantly let go. Edward glanced at him. There were signs of bruising on his face where he had hit him earlier and the fact he had left marks pleased him. He returned his gaze to Sophia.

"I saw you earlier," he confessed, "in your room with him."

Apart from Sarah, everyone could go to hell as far as Edward was concerned and he felt he had nothing to lose. Lets see her talk her way out of this.

"He undressed you,"

For a third time in minutes a wave of shocked murmurs reverberated around the room at the accusation.

"The boy's gone mad," remarked Mrs Holland in the background.

For a split second Mrs Carter glowered at him with venom in her eyes before switching her persona to a shocked and innocent one. She forced a wry laugh and glanced back at her employees for a second.

"Nonsense," she chuckled, "Marie hasn't left my side since we came back from riding,"

She turned back to face Edward and her smile dropped like a stone. Her face was like thunder. "Did he undress her too?" she snarled.

Edward arched his eyebrows.

"I never said when I saw you," he commented, sneeringly.

It was then that Sophia remembered Sarah. She was still sitting on the bed behind Edward and she had witnessed her response to Edward's comments, seen her expressions change as she hid her true feelings from everyone else.

Thinking quickly she addressed her to stave off suspicion.

"I have no idea where this is coming from," she said, pleadingly, "Sarah, please, tell the boy to stop this."

Sarah did not reply and it was Albert who eventually stepped forward to her rescue. He turned to face the group and suggested that everyone returned to their duties while the boy calmed down.

"No one will ever speak of this again," he added, "The boy's clearly still upset about his father's passing and doesn't know what he's saying."

Sarah stood next to Edward and put her hand on his shoulder.

"Enough's enough. Edward," she said, softly, "Let it go."

Albert's intervention had given DaSilva time to think. It was a perfect opportunity to destroy the boys story once and for all.

"I know where thees anger comes from," he announced.

All eyes turned to him.

"He theenks I killed his papa."

Sarah asked Edward if it was true and the boy glared at DaSilva.

"And all thees rage is aimed at me," added the slimy man.

"I've heard enough," said Albert intervening, "Everyone back to their duties this instant."

One by one they left the room talking among themselves as they went but Sophia, DaSilva and Sarah remained behind. Edward and DaSilva were still glaring at each other.

"You murdered him alright," growled Edward, once Albert had closed the door behind him, "and I know why."

Recalling Edward's comment about Marie a

few moments ago Sophia was keen for nothing more to be said in front of Sarah. The boy had been right about her undressing in front of Armando, she had no idea how he knew, and she felt he was about to bring Marie into his accusations.

"I want to talk to Edward alone," she demanded.

She gave Armando a stern look before glancing more kindly at Sarah. DaSilva didn't want to leave her alone with the boy but she pointed out that, after such a public scene, he was unlikely to do anything to her and that she would be perfectly fine.

Edward asked Sarah to leave and with a kiss to his cheek she did but DaSilva stood fast for a short while longer. Their eyes had not unlocked since everyone had left.

"Armando!" snapped Sophia.

Eventually, DaSilva averted his glare and held out his open hand towards Edward. The shiny black button rested in his palm.

"Yours I believe," he sneered.

Edward looked at it. He remembered snagging his jacket on the frame of the vent and he knew the instant he saw the button that Lisa had not accused him. However, he was too fired up to accept anything from that bastard and he angrily knocked it to the ground.

DaSilva never flinched, instead he simply smirked at Edward before leaving his room and closing the door.

14

Mrs Carter sauntered over to the dormer window and watched Armando make his way across the courtyard. Edward watched her hatefully but said nothing. She took her time scanning the manor house opposite as she chose her next words carefully.

"I don't know what you saw, or think you saw," she said eventually, " but there's nothing going on between Armando and I."

"I know what I saw,"

She turned to face him.

"And heard," he added, spitefully.

She took a moment as she tried to recall what had been said at the time of her, indiscretion. The boy's father had been mentioned but the exact conversation was vague.

"Look!" she snapped, "It makes no difference what was said, after this little fiasco, who'll believe you?"

Edward sat on the edge of his bed. "Mr Carter might."

"But, you've no proof. It's just hear say!" she said, smirking.

Edward huffed. "The whole house just witnessed DaSilva almost strangle me for a pair of tights," he retorted, "Why react like that if there's nothing to hide?"

Sophia struggled to answer for a moment, tripping over her words.

"You no longer have the stockings besides, everyone knows they weren't mine," she said, finally, "and that's what they'll say in my defence."

Sophia was right. The stockings were no longer viable for his argument against them. They may have helped to sow a little doubt, but without any more evidence his story was dead in the water.

"Then, what did you mean by, *You sure he doesn't suspect anything else*?" asked Edward trying a new tack, hoping to trip her up.

Sophia frowned. "I don't know what you mean." she answered, looking unsure of herself.

"Sure you do. DaSilva said that I suspected him of murdering my dad and you said, *Are you sure he doesn't suspect anything else*?"

Edward stared into her eyes. "What did you mean by that?"

Mrs Carter pursed her lips as she glared down at the boy. He was a cunning devil and she knew he wanted to trick her into saying too much, but why? There was no one around to hear her confess and it would be her word against his.

She was beginning to lose her patience.

"What do you think I meant?" she bawled.

Edward smiled. She had not denied the accusation and, by asking him that question, she had actually reinforced it, and she knew it. Her eyes narrowed.

"My dad was murdered because he found out

Marie is not your husbands daughter."

Sophia gasped. "That's absurd!" she snapped, "Course she's his daughter."

Edward shook his head. "I don't think so," he said, sternly, "and neither did my dad and that's why you had DaSilva kill him."

She stepped forward and slapped Edward across his face.

"You've gone too far, Edward" she yelled, flaring her nostrils, "Have you any idea what he'd do to me if you were to spread shit like that? And not just to me."

"But, is it true?"

"No."

Just then they heard the stairs creak and their eyes flashed towards the door, a moment later in walked Mr Carter followed closely by DaSilva. He had heard raised voices as he ascended the stairs and asked his wife what was going on.

"I leave the house for a minute and all hell breaks loose," he added.

"He walked in on the staff talking," DaSilva informed them, "and I told him that Edward had been caught roaming the house."

Edward wasn't surprised that he had left out the thieving part. All this fuss over a pair of stockings, what would Mr Carter think?

William stepped towards them.

"Why is his face and neck red?" he enquired, looking first at the mark Sophia had left only seconds before and then at the ones DaSilva had inflicted. It was then that he noticed the bruising on DaSilva's cheekbone as he looked back at him questioningly.

"Put up a fight did he?" he enquired, disdainfully, "perhaps I should enter him into the contest instead."

DaSilva managed a wry smile but said nothing and William looked back at Sophia.

"Don't you think you've over reacted?" he asked, staring at her sternly, "The boy's been in the house, big deal. Dock a few meals or have him scrub the floors or something."

He looked down at Edward and at his red face as he continued. "you don't beat him up and get the staff involved for something so trivial."

Sophia raised her eyebrows but said nothing. Mr Carter frowned at her silence, he was beginning to realise that their behaviour was odd. He had heard her shouting on his way in but now she appeared sheepish, almost ashamed, and Edward had not said a word or even looked at him.

"Or is there something you're not telling me?"

Sophia glared at Edward for a moment before forcing another one of her false smiles and transforming into someone else in a blink of an eye.

"No. You're right, I've over reacted," she confessed, "The whole thing got out of hand and we got carried away."

"We?"

"Armando and I."

Mr Carter sighed deeply as he tried to keep his composure. He was a man of little patience and hated being lied to. Sophia could tell he did not believe her, she knew the signs well, and needed to quell any suspicion.

"Isn't that right, Edward?" she asked with pleading eyes.

Edward looked up at her. Her demeanour had changed. She was no longer the confident matriarch but more a nervous criminal awaiting her sentence. He had the power to bring her world crashing down around her, and she knew it.

One word from him and that would be that. He wouldn't need proof, the mere suggestion of infidelity would be enough to send William into a murderous rage. But Edward felt reluctant to spill the beans, there was Marie to think about. The consequences for her would be devastating.

"That's right," offered Armando, feeling that the boy had taken too long to answer, "We got eento a scuffle and one theeng led to another."

"Edward?" Mr Carter asked, also feeling that the boy had hesitated too long. He was not prepared to accept DaSilva's explanation.

Eventually, Edward averted his gaze from Mrs to Mr Carter.

"I wanted to see the stained glass windows on the landing and ended up hiding from everyone," he explained, "and then I got caught."

Sophia held her breath and looked at her husband. Edward's story had sounded plausible enough, surely he'd bought it.

William stared down at the boy for a few moments before looking directly at his wife. It was out of character for her to involve herself in anything other than self indulgence or Marie and her presence here had vexed him.

"And the scuffle attracted the attention of the staff?" he enquired of her.

His wife nodded.

"And you felt it necessary to intervene?"

Again, she nodded.

William pondered for a second or two as he looked at each of them in turn. It just wasn't like her to be bothered with something like this, the whole thing felt contrived. They were hiding something from him and he hated it.

"Very well," he said, still unconvinced at the truth of the matter, "Now that you've resolved the issue you can go back to the manor, yes?"

Mrs Carter agreed with him immediately and with a simple, yet meaningful, glance in Edward's direction, she left the bedroom followed closely by DaSilva. Edward felt that the conversation was to be continued.

Mr Carter stood motionless for a couple of seconds as he looked down at Edward who did his best to appear unperturbed. He could tell that the man was mulling over the incident in his head and that it hadn't sat comfortably for him. He felt something was amiss and Edward knew that any doubt William had now could be useful if needed in the future.

"Is there anything going on that I should know about, Edward?" Mr Carter asked, solemnly.

Edward faked innocence and shook his head.

"Are you sure boy?"

"Yes, sir."

Suddenly, Mr Carter pounced towards the dormer and flung open the window. He shouted down and told Sophia to wait for him there and a sly exchange of words between her and DaSilva as they parted did not go unnoticed.

Edward had not seen what Mr Carter had just witnessed but he could tell that he was not happy with whatever it was. The man turned to face him, his eyes glaring.

"If I find out you've kept something from me, Edward" he snarled.

And with that he left the room.

15

Edward felt a little awkward at breakfast the next morning. Like the day before, he was the last to arrive but this time no one looked at him when he entered the kitchen.

He sat down beside Lisa and Sarah slid him a plate of bacon and eggs. He thanked her with a smile and she acknowledged him with a smile back but she never spoke.

He glanced around at the others as he helped himself to the toast but all eyes were fixed firmly on their plates. He could tell that they had been talking about him but the conversation would have ended with the creaky step.

"I didn't kill anyone," he said, trying to break the ice.

Dawson finally looked up from his breakfast.

"We're disappointed with you, son," he said, "Stealing from DaSilva and letting young Lisa here take the blame, it's not right."

"But I told her to blame me," confessed Edward, gazing at Lisa, "Didn't I, I said put the blame on me, didn't I?"

Lisa blanked him and continued to eat.

"But she thought you were doing it to help her," Stefan remarked, "You left out the part where you were actually the guilty one."

Edward sighed and hung his head.

"I know and I'm truly sorry for that, but I had my reasons for not wanting to involve her," he explained, glancing at her again, "Offering to take the blame was the next best thing."

"And what reasons might they be?" Dawson pried, before taking a gulp of tea, "That conspiracy theory of yours by any chance?"

Edward did not answer at first, instead he took a few bites of food to think of a reply. It was obvious that no one believed what he had said and that was probably for the best. After all, he had no intention of involving anyone but DaSilva in his revenge plan and it was he who had created the situation.

"It was DaSilva who caused a scene, not me" he said eventually, "If he'd confronted me alone then none of this would've happened."

Sarah clattered the pans angrily into the sink.

"If you hadn't stolen from him, Edward, "she said sternly, "He wouldn't have confronted you."

Edward said nothing and continued to eat.

"You can't blame others for your actions," she added.

"Sarah's right son," Dawson remarked, "You were the cause of it all."

Not wanting to be left out Stefan agreed with him.

Finishing off her food Lisa placed her knife and fork on the plate and began to drink her tea. Edward apologised once more and she looked into his eyes.

"I guess you were willing to take the blame for me and for that I'm grateful," she said softly, "You didn't have to and at least you had given me a way out, even if your button hadn't been found."

Edward thanked her for being so understanding.

"But, I wish you'd just told me the truth from the start." she added.

Edward agreed.

"Alone?" enquired Stefan, interrupting.

Edward raised his eyebrows at the question as he swallowed his food.

"You said that if he had confronted you alone?"

Edward nodded.

"You make it sound as though you'd planned it?"

Again, Edward nodded. "But I hadn't planned on having an audience."

Dawson huffed. "Planned it my arse," he retorted, "What happened yesterday was a damn fiasco. Planned it."

Edward didn't like being called a liar, not by anyone. Although he had not foreseen the exact outcome he had expected a reaction from DaSilva. He knew that as soon as he had told Lisa to blame him a confrontation was inevitable.

Edward shrugged his shoulders.

"Believe what you will, but you all know what you saw," he said, preparing another forkful of bacon, "He almost killed me over a pair of stockings."

Dawson sat quietly for a moment as he recalled the incident. DaSilva's finger marks were still visible on the lad's throat and he had to agree that the man had overreacted.

"The question you all need to ask yourselves is, why?" added Edward, talking with his mouth full, "and why did Mrs Carter seem anxious to prove that the stockings weren't hers even before I'd made any accusation?"

At that moment the door to the kitchen was opened and Albert stood on the threshold, stern faced. Edward had not heard the front door open and wondered how long the old man had been listening.

He nodded in acknowledgement of their greetings before asking Lisa to attend to her duties. She did as she was told without hesitation but paused briefly to smile at Edward before leaving. Edward's heart skipped a beat and he knew she had forgiven him. Albert clenched his teeth in annoyance.

"Is the bell pull not working?" enquired Dawson, wondering why the man had made a special journey over.

"In light of recent events," he announced, ignoring Dawson completely, "It has been decided that Edward be confined to his room and not allowed out unaccompanied."

Edward looked at the two men across the table and Dawson arched his eyebrows at him and pursed his lips as if to say, *'I saw that coming'.*

Sarah had quietly collected some of the breakfast plates and was washing them in the sink but as Albert began to leave she spoke.

"You'd have thought that the boy's been punished enough," she said, calmly, "what with him being throttled an'all."

Albert hovered in the hallway.

"It was not my decision, Sarah," he said, keeping his back to her.

"What ever would Child Welfare say?"

Albert lingered a while longer as a he thought of a reply.

"Well, if I were you I would look for employment elsewhere before you asked them," he said coldly, and he closed the door on his way out.

"You've certainly arrived with a bang, Edward," Stefan remarked, passing Sarah his plate, "and no mistake. What else you got planned cuz this'll take some beating?"

Dawson prodded the Scott with his elbow.

"Don't encourage the lad," he barked, "he needs to keep his head down now and let the dust settle."

Edward sighed as he pushed his empty plate towards Stefan. He would have given anything to have been able to spy on them yesterday after the ruckus. He wondered what had been said, what lies Sophia had spun Mr Carter and if she and DaSilva had managed to have words afterwards.

There was no doubt in his mind. He had missed a golden chance to have gained more information. They were bound to have revealed more about the secret that they were both desperate to keep hidden.

"Never mind, Edward," said Sarah, finishing off the dishes, "It's my half day today so we can spend some time together if you want?"

Edward smiled and nodded but his thoughts were elsewhere. He was wondering if he could force one or two of those slats free from the Louvre and return to the twitten.

16

Once back in his room, Edward made straight for the sloping window and looked out onto the roof. He was eager to see how far the tall wall was from the eaves of the barn.

"I knew it," he said to himself, as he saw that the step down was only a couple of feet. "Easy."

He knew that the wall was linked to the flat roof extension of the manor house and that it would give him direct access to the large wooden vents. Now all he needed was something to help him force the slats.

Again, he remembered the key Dawson had given him to the tool shed and he rooted it from his pocket, however, he was going to have to wait until dark. Dawson and Stefan were still down stairs and Sarah would be back for that one-to-one just after lunch.

He could jump down onto the wall right now and run down it to the end of the garden but the chances of being seen during the day were too high. He had given the downpipe a thought but had decided it was too risky.

There was nothing he could do for now so he spent the next few hours tidying his room, going through his belongings and finding a place for everything as he waited for Sarah to get back.

The afternoon was spent watching television

with her and chatting about this and that, both doing their best to avoid bringing up the scuffle with DaSilva the previous evening. They managed to finish a half completed jigsaw puzzle that had lay on a side table for weeks and they got to know each other a little better.

It turned out to be a good bonding session for both of them and the day ended with her running him a bath and making them both a bite to eat.

At last, he was alone in his room and it was dark outside. He got dressed, propped a chair beneath the door handle to prevent anyone entering and carefully climbed out onto the roof. Sarah had never bothered him before after lights out and he saw no reason why she would tonight, after all, they'd spent all afternoon together but, better safe than sorry.

The night air was chilly and Edward could feel a few spots of rain on his face. The slates were slippery and creaked with every step but he managed to crab-walk his way precariously towards the gable end. Before long he was standing on the uneven slabs of the wall looking back at the house.

With no one in sight he made his way down to the end of the garden wall. The full moon, peering through gaps in the clouds, was a welcome friend and it allowed him to see where he was going especially when the wall stepped down in several places.

Soon he had reached the bottom and he hung from the slabs and dropped to the ground. The wall here was higher than he had imagined and he knew it would not be easy getting back up, especially laden with tools.

Keeping close to the wall he ran back towards the tool shed. A couple of bedroom lights were still on and he crept as quietly as he could as he neared the building. He pulled his dad's flashlight from his rucksack and gripped it in his teeth as he opened the padlock.

The door moaned as he opened it and he paused for a moment as he waited for a reaction above. It seamed to Edward that the quieter he wanted to be the louder he was.

He searched the tool shed with the torch and carefully collected the tools he thought were best for the job. A crowbar was his first choice followed by a set of chisels and then a wooden mallet.

He put the chisels and mallet in his rucksack, replaced the padlock and then made his way back down to the bottom end of the wall. He had already planned on how he would scale back up it while still in the shed.

Gripping the crowbar by the straight end, he stretched up his arm and then jumped as high as he could. It took him several attempts but soon he had hooked the curved end onto the slabs and was hanging a couple feet off the ground by one hand.

With great effort he managed to pull himself up the bar and before too long he was making his way towards the manor house. The metal bar had made some noise as it clanked off the wall but he was sure he was far enough away for anyone to have heard it.

He crept onto the flat roof and tiptoed passed the large glass lantern, peering down into the room below as he went. The roofing felt crunched a little underfoot and he hoped that it had not betrayed him.

With his adrenalin pumping Edward eventually reached his goal and immediately set about removing the bottom two slats. Wedging the crowbar between them he pushed with all his might but at first nothing happened. It was raining a little harder now and the slats were getting slippery.

He tried the other end and was pleased to see it move slightly as it slid inwards. Encouraged, he returned to the other end and did the same to that. Moving from one side to the other many times he finally managed to coax the first slat free.

Now that he knew the method the second slat was removed in half the time and he was soon able to squeeze himself once more into the secret twitten. Using a chisel from his rucksack he shaved down one end of both slats so that he could replace and remove them easily. He was now able to come and go whenever he pleased at night.

Leaving the tools Edward made his way towards DaSilva's room using the flashlight muffled by one of his socks. He couldn't risk the light being seen through the vents and had to keep it to a minimum, just enough to see with.

He knew that the probability of learning anything new tonight was slim but he wanted to spy on Armando all the same. He knew his best bet of getting him to talk was to upset him again, get him worked up enough to go crying to Sophia. She was sure to go mad and reveal more about their secret.

Edward's field of view was obscured slightly by a coat hanging on the back of a chair but he could see Armando clear enough through the vent. The half dressed hit man was sitting at his dressing table and appeared to be cleaning something metallic.

Edward was much lower than the tabletop and had to wait for DaSilva to pick up the items for him to see but it soon became apparent as to what he was cleaning. He began using a wiry pipe cleaner on the barrel of a pistol.

The boy watched the man skilfully reassemble the gun in seconds, cock it and pull the trigger at himself in the mirror. It wasn't hard to imagine him shooting his dad. The Portuguese slime bag certainly knew what he was doing.

Edward hung around just long enough to see where he stashed the gun. It was getting late and he was worried that Sarah had tried the door. He made his way back to the Louvre, collected the tools and squeezed himself out between the slats.

They slotted back into place like a glove and he

congratulated himself for the fine job he had done as he crept back across the flat roof. He passed the glass lantern, hopped onto the wall and hurried back to the barn, glancing back occasionally to check that the coast was clear.

He clambered onto the roof. It was still spitting and Edward slipped several times on the wet slates as he made his way back to the sloping window. It had been a precarious undertaking but one he felt was worth the risk. He knew that the tools needed to be replaced at some point but would have to wait for the right opportunity to arise. For now he slid them under his bed and retired for the evening, eager for his next visit to the secret passage.

17

The next morning Dawson went over the tasks for the week ahead with Edward during breakfast. It was Monday and his first day on the job.

"There'll be a bit of everything this week," he explained, talking with his mouth full, "Branch lopping, hedge trimming, slabbing but we'll start with that flowerbed wall, how are you at mixing cement?"

Edward shrugged his shoulders, "I guess we'll find out," he answered.

It was another chilly morning but at least the rain had stopped. They trudged around to the back of the barn and Dawson pulled an old wheelbarrow out of the lean-to next to the locked tool shed before removing the padlock.

He handed the lad a shovel. "Fill the barrow with sand," he instructed, before looking for what else they may need for the job, "make sure there's no bricks in it."

There was a mound of sand to the side of the lean-to and Edward filled the barrow. He was hoping that the tools he'd taken wouldn't be missed and was relieved when Dawson finally emerged from the shed with everything he needed for the job in hand.

By this time the barrow was almost full and Dawson threw the tools on top and asked the lad to follow him. Edward pushed the heavy barrow to the first stable from where Dawson emerged with a dry bag of cement, which was also loaded onto the barrow.

The man also filled a bucket with water from an outside tap and from there they made their way to the flowerbed wall.

Edward was glad to see that Dawson was a methodical worker, in that he did not rush things, he prepared well for a job and thought of everything he needed before hand to avoid running back and forth.

The whole week was the same. The flowerbed wall was repaired on the Monday, a few slabs were relayed on the Tuesday, they trimmed the hedges on the Wednesday and so on. *"A job a day,"* was Dawson's motto and it suited Edward just fine. It gave them time to chat and they were usually finished by early afternoon.

He didn't see much of Albert or his wife during the week and only saw Lisa at breakfast or in the evening for a short while but he did see Connor several times who had waved and smiled at him.

Each evening when everyone had retired, Edward would make his secret trip across to the twitten in the hope of learning something new but always retuned disappointed. The problem was that the Carter's went to bed almost as early as everyone else. The house was always quiet with nothing to see.

However, on the Friday evening his luck

changed.

He had seen Connor pull into the driveway just as they were clearing up after fixing the garage roof. A large fat man accompanied by a painfully thin, haggard looking, woman emerged from the limo and were greeted at the portico by Sophia.

They looked foreign and Edward had assumed that they were her relations, her parents perhaps or an uncle and aunt. A second car, a long white limousine, arrived shortly afterwards.

Dawson's persona changed the moment he spotted it and he rushed Edward away, taking him back to the barn through the rear garden instead of going around the front as they normally would. Edward had not had chance to see the new arrivals.

"Is something wrong?" he enquired, struggling to keep a hold on a half roll of roofing felt.

Dawson did not answer him until they had made their way across the garden and through the gate in the courtyard wall.

"There's a contest being held here in a couple of weeks," he informed the lad as he unlocked the tool shed, "and they must be here to go over the details."

Edward felt that Dawson hadn't answered his question, he already knew about the fighting competition and was more interested why Dawson looked so worried about it.

"Is that a bad thing?" Edward asked, looking puzzled, "You're acting like it is."

Dawson threw the tools back in the shed

without answering and replaced the padlock. His usual smiling eyes were now sullen and staring.

"Who are they?" Edward enquired, sternly, "Why are you so afraid?"

Dawson huffed and marched off without reply, Edward was forced to trot after him.

"Dawson, who are they?"

"They're bad news," said the sinewy man, "Just keep out of sight while they're here."

"But, why?"

Dawson glowered at him. There was concern in his eyes but, concern for who?

"Just do it Edward," he said solemnly.

Edward felt that Dawson's woefulness was for him and was beginning to feel a little uncomfortable. A sense of foreboding, a growing feeling of something unpleasant about to happen was taking hold. Was he in danger?

"Are they staying?" he enquired.

"I wouldn't have thought so. Not tonight," Dawson answered as he guided the lad back to the barn, "But they'll be staying here soon enough, I'm sure."

They kicked off their shoes and headed into the kitchen. Dawson began making them both a hot drink while Edward sat at the table and removed his work coat Sarah had given him. He was intrigued to know who the strangers were and why Dawson was so agitated at their arrival. He was hoping that they'd still be there on his nightly visit to the twitten.

"There's no need to worry about me," said Edward, nonchalantly, "I can look after myself you know."

Dawson looked down at the lad and smiled as he waited for the kettle to boil. The boy did look a lot like his father, Gareth Kane, and he already had his sturdy build. There was still some growing to do but the boy was strong and his father was sure to have taught him a thing or two about hand to hand combat.

"I don't doubt it." he said, "but I still think it's best you stay out of sight."

"You know I'll find out who they are sooner or later so, you may as well tell me now to avoid my curiosity getting the better of me."

The grounds man thought for a moment. The lad was the type to take matters in his own hands, his recent behaviour proved that, and was likely to go out of his way to find out who they are. Keeping the information from him was simply fuelling the fire.

"Very well," he said eventually, with a heavy sigh, "The fat guy and the rake of a woman are Mrs Carter's brother and sister in-law. They're here from Portugal and will probably be staying a couple of weeks."

Dawson continued to make the tea as he explained.

"He's the one who inherited the shipping company from their dad."

"And the people from the white limo?" Edward

interrupted. He had already assumed as much about the fat dude, he was more interested in the others. The one's that the grounds man felt were a danger to him.

Dawson eventually sat down at the table and slid Edward a cup of hot tea.

"That was Mr Billingham. He owns probably the second largest haulage company in the country, next to 'Carter's Cargo' that is, and I assume he's here to re-enter the competition."

"Re-enter?"

Dawson nodded and sipped his tea as he chose how to continue.

"Two years ago his brother, first time in the contest, suffered a brain bleed after he was knocked out cold in the ring. He lost the use of one arm and doesn't know who he is any more. As you can imagine, tempers flared back then and Billingham swore revenge on the man who did it, especially as he was so well trained"

"My dad?"

Dawson nodded.

"You see, it's supposed to be an amateur contest but they accused Gareth of being a professional."

Edward shook his head. "But, he was self taught." he added.

"Yes, but they were having none of it."

"So, what happened?"

"Well, they're a nasty bunch you see, and I heard that everyone had expected some kind of retaliation for months afterwards but they ended up simply withdrawing from future contests."

"And now that my dad's gone, they.........." Edward's words tapered off.

"Exactly."

There was a pause in the conversation as Dawson drank his tea.

"And you think if he finds out I'm here he'll.............." again, Edward's words tapered off.

Dawson nodded.

"There's only two reasons why he's here in my mind," offered Dawson, "One. He feels the contest is open again and his guy stands a chance of winning or, two.............." It was Dawson's turn to taper off his sentence.

"Or two," Edward added, continuing for him, "He knows I'm here."

18

It seemed to take an age for the evening to roll by and Edward was beginning to think the clock had stopped. To add to his frustration everyone hung around longer than usual and seemed reluctant to turn in.

Dawson had asked him not to mention Mr Billingham but a large part of the conversation topic was about the rapidly approaching contest. Lisa was especially excited about the prospect of seeing grown men pummel one and other but was disappointed when Sarah pointed out that she would not be allowed in. Embarrassed, she was the first to go to bed.

It was agreed that Connor would probably be Mr Carter's choice for his champion. The man was a bruiser and had trained with Gareth on occasion, been in the army with him and had fought at his side.

Edward was told that each company entered two contestants and was surprised to learn that DaSilva had entered every one of them as Mr Carter's number two. He had even come close a few times of reaching the final but had lost in the semi's and to his dad more often than not.

Edward knew that if Mr Billingham had returned just for him then there was only one person responsible for it, DaSilva. The 'would be hit man' loathed him and would jump at the chance of getting rid of him.

What puzzled Edward was he could not see how Billingham could possibly take his revenge out on him. After all, it was not as though he would be fighting in the contest.

At last, everyone had gone to bed and Edward hung around for a short while longer before clambering out onto the roof. He was glad to see that there were still lights on in the manor as he made his way towards it.

He crept across the flat roof and peered down onto the lounge. He could see several people sitting around a large coffee table deep in conversation and there were two young lads playing snooker behind them.

They were both in their late teens or early twenties, one was quite stocky with long hair but the other was taller with a more athletic build and a crew cut. Edward couldn't help but wonder if they were part of DaSilva's plan. He sensed they were there for a reason.

Billingham was talking to DaSilva on the sofa. The man had a beard that looked ginger in places and he kept stroking his hand down it as he talked. His shirt sleeves were rolled up revealing heavily tattooed arms and his collar was undone to show off a chunky gold necklace. Large gold rings on both hands glinted in the lamplight. He reminded Edward of a gypsy, carrying his wealth around with him.

Sophia was talking to her brother. The portly man was sunk deep into an armchair and was sipping something from a large round glass. His wife was sat next to DaSilva and was reading from a magazine. Her expression was one of mild indignation.

Edward left them to it and quietly made his way to the Louvre. He clambered into the secret passage and carefully replaced the slats. As he had all week he paused for a moment at the landing vent to peer out at the arched windows. It had become a nightly ritual for him that he felt obliged to keep up.

For the first time that week Edward found Sophia's room unoccupied and was not going to waste a perfect opportunity a have a rummage around.

Carefully, he unclipped the vent cover and placed it on the carpet before heaving himself out into the bedroom. The door was slightly ajar and the voices were a distant hum, barely audible but reassuringly far enough away.

He scanned the room with the torch, un-socked. With no idea of what he was looking for he searched the drawers and wardrobes. If only he could find more proof of their adultery or something he could use against them.

He came across Sophia's stocking drawer and examined them for that famous label Mrs Simpson had made a point to mention.

What did she say again? *"Yours have a white label."*

Edward carefully unfolded one of them and was disappointed to find that they did indeed have a tiny white makers tag on the inside. He did his best to replace it as neatly as possible and continued his search.

As he rummaged through her jewellery boxes he came across a gold ring with a large amethyst that reminded him of his mother. She used to have one just like it and the more he rummaged the more items he found that looked very familiar. A distinctive necklace and a wristwatch.

Suddenly, his mind flashed back to when he was sitting in the limousine. Mrs Carter was messing with her rings while Mr Carter gave him the third degree. He had sensed at the time that something felt odd about her and now he knew what it was, her rings. She had turned them to hide the stones.

He'd recognised them without actually realising it. The rings once belonged to his mother but how and why did Sophia have them?

An icy chill ran up his spine as he looked down at his mom's jewellery. Something was already telling him that he was not going to like the answer. Surely it belonged to him now, not some sleaze-bag. Edward couldn't believe that his dad would just give them to her, but how else would she have them?

"Did he love her or something?"

Just then, and only for a moment the voices down stairs were louder than usual as a door was opened and closed. He had no time to ponder further on why the jewellery was there, someone was coming and he had to get out.

He darted for the vent, climbing through and replaced it just as the lights were switched on. It was Sophia and she looked a little drunk as she sauntered towards the bed.

Edward watched as she ferreted through her handbag, empty something white from a small bottle across the back of her hand and then inhale it with one loud sniff.

As he watched her he wrestled with the idea of her and his father. He hated her and the fact that she had his mother's jewellery. How could his dad have done such a terrible thing? To give another woman your dead wife's belongings meant that there were feelings there of some descript, a desire, a want. But what did it mean?

"Were they having an affair?"

Suddenly, he remembered Marie and his suspicions of her not being Mr Carter's daughter. He had assumed that she could be DaSilva's but was now having second thoughts. He began to feel nauseous.

"Is Marie dad's daughter?"

Edward knew he could be jumping to conclusions again but was struggling to think of another reason why Sophia had his mom's things. His dad must have given them to her, there was no other explanation.

He wondered if his mom had known about them and if it had something to do with her leaving so abruptly. Could it also be responsible for her death. It was then that a sinister and unthinkable thought materialised and his eyes filled with tears.

"Not my mom! No, dad wouldn't."

A mans voice grabbed his attention and he sprang back to the vent, wiping his eyes. The voice was unmistakable, DaSilva had sneaked into her room.

"I thought you'd given that up," he hissed, grabbing the handbag from her aggressively, "Don't you theenk eets caused me enough trouble?"

Sophia was too wasted to stop him but she lifted her up head and laughed at him.

"You trouble?" she questioned, flopping her head back down on the mattress, "I'm the one who suffered."

Armando peered down the corridor before rummaging through her bag. He stuffed the small bottle into his pocket.

"Thees fucking stuff has cost us both," he whispered angrily, "No more."

Again, Sophia laughed.

"You gave it me."

"No," snarled DaSilva, nearing the bed, "I gave eet you once. What happened all those years ago ees on you!"

There was a long silence and Edward thought

Sophia had fallen to sleep but then she spoke.

"Don't you think I know that?" she sobbed, "Why do you think I still take it?"

"Because you're weak!"

Sophia shot up and glared at him, her expression was one of both surprise and self pity. Unable to hold her position for long, she flopped back down on the bed without responding.

"I suffer too but you don't see me numbing myself with eet." added DaSilva, peering through the door again for anyone approaching, "Who's the supplier?"

The distant hum of voices could still be heard and he felt confident enough to hang around a little longer.

Again, Sophia paused for a while before eventually telling him to mind his own business.

"How long have you been using?"

With no reply offered, Armando marched over to the bed and lurched over his cousin with his hands to either side of her chest.

"How long?" he asked again.

Sophia giggled and put her arms around his neck. Slowly, she pulled him closer until they were almost kissing.

"Must we fight, Armi?" she teased.

For a moment, DaSilva let their lips touch. Edward could see he wanted to respond but somehow managed to resist. Eventually, he pushed himself off the bed.

"Damn it, Soph, eet's already taken a life" he

said, wiping her lipstick from his mouth, "Eef he ever found out he'd keel us both. You have to stop thees."

Just then the guests spilled out into the hallway below and DaSilva was forced to retreat, darting from the room like a man demented.

Edward pondered for a while on what they had said as he watched Sophia clumsily making herself ready for bed. She had a drug problem that went back a while, that much he had gathered. DaSilva had supplied it to her once but she continued to dull her senses and something happened. The question there was what?

It was difficult for him to pick the bones out of anything they had said, his mind was still in shock with the possibility that his dad may have killed his mom for that incestuous bitch.

He couldn't believe he was thinking such a terrible thing. And to think, they were buried in the same grave. Edward slid down the wall on to his bottom. His world was in tatters.

"How could you," he sobbed, quietly.

19

It was getting late by the time Edward had made his way back to his room. He had been thinking about the jewellery and what he'd witnessed between the kissing cousins. There were more questions than answers and he was confused and upset.

However, by the time he had changed into his pyjamas he had convinced himself that he had jumped to conclusions. There was no way his dad would have killed his mom and he had too much respect for Mr Carter to have had an affair with his wife. His dad had always been a man of principal and would never do anything he wouldn't like done to himself.

There had to be another reason why that bitch had his mom's jewellery. He was struggling to think of one at the moment but it didn't mean there wasn't one. He thought it over as he got ready for bed.

A pencil on the small bedside table gave him an idea. With his mind in over-drive he needed clarity. The facts were getting jumbled up and writing them down could help.

He found an old school jotter and sat up in bed for the next hour or so making notes. It soon became apparent that there were only three facts to the whole thing - both his parents had been killed, Sophia and DaSilva were hiding something about Marie and somehow Sophia had his mom's stuff. The rest he had assumed.

By watching them together, Edward knew the cousin's were lovers, or at least, had been once but he could not prove it. Their performance when he stole the stockings was odd and even Mr Carter was suspicious of their actions. Everyone was. Something was definitely wrong.

He could not shake the image of his dad having an affair with Sophia and his train of thought changed. Apart from the height difference, his dad and Mr Carter were very similar in facial features and hair colour. His dad had told him once that they had been mistaken for being brothers on more than one occasion.

If Marie was his father's offspring there would be no obvious signs of adultery because of their likeness but, if she was DaSilva's there might. He had black hair, dark eyes and skin and Marie did not.

Although Sophia also had olive skin her daughter had not inherited it from her, it was fair like Mr Carter's and his father's. Her hair was brown, almost rose gold in the sun, and much lighter than Sophia's auburn locks. Her blue eyes were the only thing she had inherited from Sophia. Mr Carter's were brown but his own father's were blue. Was that significant he thought?

He was adamant to disprove his assumption that Marie was his half sister but the more he examined their likeness the more it seemed the nightmare could be plausible.

It was then that another question presented itself to him.

"Why had DaSilva waited seven years to kill dad?"

That part of this dilemma was puzzling. He gave it more thought from a couple of angles, starting from his original assumption that Marie was not Mr Carter's daughter and he refused to believe she was his dad's. Annoyingly, due to her not resembling him in any way at all, he had to take Armando out of the pot too. It was confusing, she had to be someone's kid. Perhaps there was a third person, someone Edward had not considered.

Something that DaSilva had mentioned earlier, when confronting Sophia about the drugs, somehow squeezed its way into his thoughts.

"What happened all those years ago is on you." he had said.

That would imply that he had known about Marie for a long time before murdering his dad, assuming that that was what he was referring to.

"It's already taken a life," was another thing that had come from that murdering bastard's lips. What had he meant by that?

Thinking more clearly, Edward played back their full conversation in his head. The drugs had caused a lot of trouble for DaSilva a few years ago and Sophia was still tormented by what had happened. They were definitely covering something up, that he was sure of.

From that moment he swore to himself never to jump to conclusions again. There had to be another reason why that lousy cow had the jewellery and he knew that he had only got half the story, broken snippets of hearsay.

Besides, it wasn't all her jewellery, just some of it, so where was the rest? Like a lightening bolt he suddenly remembered his dad's strong box. He had installed it in the pantry floor and hidden it beneath the linoleum. He used to put their valuables in it whenever they went on holiday to save taking too much with them. The rest of her things must be in there.

He scrambled out of bed and retrieved a cardboard box from the bottom of his small wardrobe. He rummaged around for a while but was forced to empty it onto the floor. He was pleased to see the key among the other bits and pieces. Relieved, he climbed back into bed.

He then remembered that the house had been rented and it was sure to have new tenants by now. He was suddenly anxious that they may have discovered it and taken everything. It wasn't exactly a safe and could be opened with a few hefty hammer blows.

"I'll see Mr Carter first thing," he promised himself as he looked at his dad's watch on the bedside table.

He picked it up and smiled as he realised the time. His mother had told him he had been born at one thirty five in the morning and in exactly five seconds that would have been fourteen years ago today.

"Happy Birthday, Ed," he whispered, trying to remember the sound of her voice.

20

Edward mentioned his mom's jewellery to Sarah the next morning at breakfast once they were alone. He explained that he had been given his dad's belongings and knew about the stuff tied up in probate but that he had not been given anything of hers, apart from some old photo's. He then told her about the strong box.

"I'm sure Connor could take you back there to get it," she said, tidying up, "I'll ask Albert to mention it to Mr Carter if you like, I'm going over there now."

Edward thanked her as he helped put the breakfast things away. He was beginning to feel he could trust her but, for some reason, he kept his birthday a secret. He didn't want any fuss and definitely didn't feel like celebrating.

He stood in the barn doorway and watched Sarah make her way to the main kitchen across the courtyard. She waved at him and smiled before disappearing inside.

He returned to his room and had only been there about fifteen minutes when Lisa called to him from the small entrance hall below. Mr Carter wanted to see him straight away. News of hidden treasure had obviously sparked his interest.

He stuffed the key into his pocket and ran down to greet her. Her beaming smile and piercing blue eyes were a delight to behold as she escorted him across to the manor.

She had not been privy to what was going on and she asked Edward if he knew why he had been summoned. He told her as much as he wanted her to know while they made their way to the library.

However, they only got as far as the hallway when they came across Mr Carter. He was standing in the entrance doorway and talking to Connor, who was dressed in his chauffeur's uniform. They were clearly going out somewhere and looked annoyed at having to hang around.

"This strong box," said Mr Carter abruptly, as Edward approached, "Where is it?"

Edward had hoped that he would be able to go himself but, judging by Mr Carter's urgency to leave, he knew that wasn't going to happen.

"It's under the pantry floor," he informed him.

"Is there a key?" Mr Carter asked sharply, "a combination, what?"

The man sounded angry with him. Perhaps he had argued with Mrs Carter over the scene in his room and blamed him for it, or he still felt that Edward had kept the truth of the matter from him. Whichever it was, his hostility towards him was palpable.

"It can be carried."Edward said.

"Have you the means to open it if I bring it back?"

Edward nodded. There was no way he was giving him the key so that he could open it first.

"There's a key," he confessed, "It'll be in my room somewhere."

Mr Carter let out a loud sigh and gave Connor a knowing look.

"And you never thought to find it before bringing it up?"

Edward felt his cheeks redden with anger. The man could do with a good thump. He bit his lip.

"I didn't think it would happen this quickly," he replied, "I only mentioned it at breakfast."

Without another word the angry man left the building. Connor put on his driver's cap and smiled sympathetically at the lad before following his boss to the limousine.

Edward turned to face Lisa. She looked shocked at Mr Carter's attitude towards him and said as much as he neared her. They were on there way out when Mrs Carter called after Edward.

She was gliding down the stairs in a pink negligee with Lisa's grandmother, Mrs Simpson, in tow. Edward assumed that the old cow had informed Sophia of the strong box. She was looking smug and sanctimonious.

"A word, if I may," said Sophia, reaching the half landing.

Lisa followed Edward to the foot of the stairs but, with a nod from Mrs Carter, her grandmother hurried her away. Sophia waited for them both to disappear before speaking.

She flicked her head back to correct her posture and sniffed, self-importantly, as she prepared herself. Edward felt she was a condescending bitch who always felt a need to show how important she was. He hated her.

"Do you believe in coincidences, Edward?" she asked him, flicking her head back once more.

Edward shrugged his shoulders. "I suppose," he said, uninterestedly.

She looked at him disdainfully for a moment before asking him to follow her. She led him through the door that was opposite the dining room and across the other side of the hallway. He had not been in there before.

It turned out to be a large lounge filled with sofas and armchairs, coffee tables and ornaments on pedestals. It was a mirror image of the dining room opposite but was intended purely for relaxing. Sophia closed the door.

She noticed Edward looking around at the portraits on the walls and at the detailed plasterwork adorning the ceiling.

"I know," she said, making her way over to a drinks cabinet, "drab, isn't it? And that damn smell, the whole place could do with decorating."

She poured herself a drink and caught Edward looking at one of the many carriage clocks that were dotted around the room.

"I know, it's early," she said, making him aware she was watching him, "but what the hell."

Her negligee was almost transparent and Edward could see how her silk nightdress below it clung to her curves, her hips and breasts, her nipples. He had already seen her completely naked once but for some reason, seeing her dressed this way, seemed more appealing to him. She was in good shape.

"So, am I here for a reason, or.............?" he asked, tapering off as he shrugged his shoulders again.

She took a sip of brandy and licked her lips, as if savouring the flavour.

"What made you remember your father's strong box?" she enquired, sauntering towards him, "It seems strange you waiting so long to mention it."

"I was looking through my things and realised there was nothing of mom's there," he explained, thinking quickly, "Why?"

Sophia took another sip of brandy. She was now only a few feet away.

"Well, unlike you," she said, narrowing her eyes, "I don't believe in coincidences."

Edward cast his mind back to last night and to weather he'd left signs of him being there. He felt Sophia suspected that he had.

"What does that mean?" he asked, keeping calm.

"Oh! It's just that I find it odd you asking about your mother's jewellery on the very morning I find that someone's been messing with mine."

Edward arched his eyebrows and tried desperately to fake surprise. "That is a coincidence."

Mrs Carter glared at him before forcing a smile.

"We used to swap things occasionally," she informed him, as she ran her finger around the rim of the glass, "I won't be surprised if you find something of mine in that box."

She took another sip. "We can exchange them if you do." she added.

As she talked Edward realised something. Why it hadn't occurred to him sooner he wasn't sure but the things Sophia had of his mother's could be the ones she was wearing the day she went missing. A wristwatch, a necklace and a couple of rings. Edward went cold the instant the thought was born.

Sophia saw the boys expression change. She could tell that some part of a mental jigsaw puzzle had just fallen into place for him. His eyes were staring, darting around at the floor as he made sense of it for a moment or two. He then glared at her hatefully, accusingly.

Puzzled, she asked him what was wrong.

"Did my dad give you her jewellery?" he asked, subduing a scowl.

Edward had promised himself that he would stop jumping to conclusions but this was different. Sophia had his moms wristwatch, a watch with a cracked and worn leather strap, why on earth would she want to borrow it?

The story about swapping jewellery was just her way of explaining why it was there but Edward knew she was lying.

"No," she replied, frowning, "Why would he?"

"So, how come you have it then?"

"I just told you. We used to swap our things now and then," she answered, her cheeks beginning to redden, "You know? For a change."

"Bullshit!"

"I beg your pardon!"

"The only piece of jewellery that was found with my moms charred body was a ring with an inscription inside it," hissed Edward, "The ring that was used to identify her with. No other items were found, not even the melted remnants of them, so I ask again. How come you have the ones she was wearing?"

Sophia's eyes widened as she pointed her highly polished fingernail at him, accusingly.

"I knew you'd been in my room!" she sneered, "You're not very good at snooping are you? You may as well have left me a note!"

Edward knew there was no point in denying it, he was on to something that was worth the fall out.

"So! On what occasion did you wear my moms watch? What high end bash was that suitable for?"

Sophia scoffed and stormed back over to the drinks cabinet.

"A fancy dress party" she snarled, glancing back at him briefly, "I went as a tramp!"

There it was, her lie confirmed. The watch was worthless, so why would she borrow it?

"Did my dad give you my mom's jewellery?" he

asked again.

She clumsily poured herself another drink, spilling some onto the tray, before turning to face him. Her negligee had opened revealing just how short her nightdress was and they stared at each other for a while in silence. She sipped her brandy with no intention of answering him.

"I had thought my dad was killed because he found out Marie wasn't your husbands," Edward explained, scrutinising her expression, "I'd assumed she was Armando's but, now I think she's my dad's daughter."

Sophia refused to respond at first. She did well to hide most of her face behind the brandy glass but her eyes could not hide her feelings. She was upset. The brandy began to jump about in the glass as her hand trembled.

"DaSilva found out and killed him and that's why you're a junkie!"

"You're insane, Edward!" she growled, "Why do you persist with this fantasy of yours? You have no proof of anything."

Edward took a step nearer.

"But I do," he snarled, "My moms things, that should've been burned along with her, for one and your strange behaviour for another. Even your husband suspects something."

With tearful eyes, Sophia downed the brandy in one gulp and wiped her mouth on her sleeve.

"I have never slept with your dad!" she snapped, pouring another drink.

"Why not? You've slept with your cousin."

"And she's not Armando's." she spat.

Edward frowned. She was beginning to look tipsy. The booze and drugs from last night must still be in her system. For the first time that morning she had sounded sincere in what she had said.

He took another step closer.

"Say that again!" he ordered.

"She's not Armando's." she repeated, almost dropping the decanter.

"No, not that. The other thing. And look at me!"

Sophia, lazily turned her eyes towards him. "I have never slept with your dad." she said.

"Swear it. On Marie's life?"

She nodded, "Yes, on Marie's life. Cross my heart and hope to die."

"So, how come you have her things then?" he enquired.

Just then there was a knock on the door and Mrs Simpson entered. She looked at them both disdainfully as they stood staring at each other, she half dressed with a glass of brandy and him clenching his fists.

"Your brother is asking for you Mrs Carter." said the housekeeper.

21

They left the lounge together and Edward stood and watched as Mrs Simpson escorted Sophia back up stairs. Neither woman turned back to look at him, not once, and he was left alone, unaccompanied.

He stood there for a while deep in thought as he stared at the family portrait on the half landing. Sophia had sworn on Marie's life that she had not slept with his father and he believed her. He was pleased to hear it but, she had not explained how or why she had his mother's things.

Edward was still convinced Marie was someone else's child. He was glad she was not his dad's but, who's was she? He had come to the manor house wanting revenge for his father's murder but now found himself wanting revenge for his mother's too. It was all connected somehow, but how?

He could have used the opportunity to sneak back to the twitten via the under-stairs cupboard but felt he would learn nothing new and would probably end up stuck in there for the day. Besides, he had a feeling he was being watched.

Instead of walking through the manor house to get back to the barn, via the kitchen, he used the front door to exit the building. Sarah and Mrs Holland had seen him earlier with Lisa and he was in no mood to answer questions.

It was nice to feel the sun on his face as he emerged from beneath the portico. It had broken through a gap in the bubbling clouds and he stood still for a moment soaking it in.

He felt relieved that his dad had not fathered Marie because there was no longer a reason why he would have murdered his mom. That thought had been making him ill and, at least, he could now push it aside. The reason he had been killed is because he had found out about Marie just as Edward had originally assumed.

As he let his mind roam he made his way across to the statue of cupid. The sound of the gravel crunching under foot was strangely satisfying and the smell of wet grass was a welcome change from the damp, musty, odour of the manor house.

He looked at the figure with his bow for a minute or two before sitting on the dwarf wall of the fountain and facing the house. To his surprise, DaSilva was standing beneath the portico lighting a cigarette.

"Shit!"

For a change, the grease-ball was more casually dressed, jeans and a pullover instead of a designer suit. He took a long drag on his cigarette and flicked away the match before strolling over towards Edward.

Edward remained seated. He had no desire to show respect for the man by leaving like a mouse.

The man was a bully, a coward, who thrived on other's being afraid of him. Edward was not scared, his hate was too strong.

Armando DaSilva stood beside the lad and placed one foot onto the wall so as to rest his elbow on his knee. The pose naturally bought his head down nearer to Edward's. The man had something to say.

He took another drag and blew the smoke down into Edward's face.

"I can't wait for next weekend," he said, smugly, taking another drag.

Edward did not respond but was forced to close his eyes a little from the stinging smoke. He remained focussed on the house.

"You know, thee contest?" added DaSilva.

Again, Edward paid no attention. His throat was still hurting from their last encounter and he had no desire to make friendly small talk with the man.

DaSilva smiled as he saw the boy's resentment of him and blew more smoke in his direction to fuel his fire.

"I think thees year is going to be the best," he continued, smirking.

Edward could not resist. "And why would that be?" he asked, looking up at the man who had killed his father, "Cause my dad's not in it?"

"Maybe," replied the slimy man, still smirking."

Edward huffed belittlingly, "But, you have no chance against Connor either," he teased, daringly.

DaSilva chuckled. He knew the boy was goading him and he gave the same reply as before, "Maybe."

There was a long pause while DaSilva finished his cigarette and dropped the butt into the fountain.

"Eets a pity you'll miss eet," he said, "Confined to your room, an'all."

The man chuckled. "All alone and out of sight," he added.

Edward remembered the two lads playing snooker. DaSilva was banking on him being in his room alone while everyone else was distracted with the contest. Had he arranged for them to pay him a visit he wondered?

There was an awkward silence as DaSilva glared at him. Edward could see his hateful expression through his peripheral vision.

"Been snooping around again, I hear?" asked DaSilva, eventually.

The boy was in no mood for a full-on confrontation and he knew the least he said about the matter the less chance there was of having one.

"Deedn't learn your lesson from last time!" added the man. His tone had changed, but again, Edward remained tight lipped. DaSilva's eyes turned to menacing slits.

"I had a dog once," he explained, keeping his head close, "I had to beat eet half to death before eet learned to respect and obey me."

Edward huffed defiantly and looked directly at

him again.

"You can beat me all you want," he said, through gritted teeth, "You'll never have my respect."

His remark forced a smile from DaSilva.

"Even thee wildest of beasts can be broken, boy."

Edward was beginning to tire of the bastard's strutting and he jumped to his feet. DaSilva stood upright and they faced each other.

"And you're just a weak sapling!" added DaSilva, menacingly.

They stood toe to toe for a while, almost touching noses. Each filled with the utmost hatred for the other. Edward narrowed his eyes.

"Why don't you just kill me like you did my dad?" he snarled.

"But, I didn't,"

"What about my mom?"

For a split second, Armando looked surprised. He arched his brow and there was a pause before his answer. The question *"How had the boy jumped to that conclusion?"* visibly washed across his face.

"Again. Not guilty."

"But, Sophia has my moms jewellery?"

DaSilva shrugged, "So?"

"Things she was wearing the day she went missing!"

Another shrug of the shoulders. "That proves notheen."

"It proves she was murdered!"

"Not by me eet doesn't!"

Edward backed away. He longed for the day he would watch the life leave this man's eyes. He knew he was lying. He'd killed both his parents, or at least, had organised it but there was no tangible proof.

"You may not have pulled the trigger or lit the match but you have blood on your hands. I know it!"

DaSilva stepped towards Edward but the lad took another step backwards. His eyes were welling up.

"I can understand why you feel that way about your father's murder, I was there but, your mother's?"

"You had a hand in it alright!"

"Another fantasy."

"No! Another fact!"

DaSilva was growing tired of the boy's accusations and waved his hands at him as if pushing him away. He huffed loudly and began to walk towards the manor house.

"She got the jewellery from you?" Edward shouted.

It was DaSilva's turn to ignore questions.

"Jewellery that should have burned in the fire?"

The man continued to blank him.

"Why did you kill her?"

Armando stopped in his tracks and turned to face the boy. Through clenched teeth he warned him to keep his mouth shut.

"Why? Because it's true?" snarled Edward.

"No. Because accusations are dangerous!" DaSilva snarled back, "Thees was explained to you last time. Eet has to stop!"

Edward felt a tear trickle down his face as they stood staring at each other again. He was going to kill the bastard but, not without proof first.

"I'll never stop!" he growled, "You're guilty and I'll prove it, even if it takes my last breath to do it!"

DaSilva smiled. He liked the idea of Edward taking his last breath.

"You've already tried to prove eet once!" he sneered, "Eet was embarrassing to watch. Who'll believe anytheen you say now?"

"I only need prove it to myself!"

"Oh, and why ees that?"

"Because, unlike you, I don't kill innocent people!"

The smile fell from Armando's face. The boy had just threatened to kill him and he did well to restrain himself from lunging for his throat again. He remained calm, bit his tongue and walked away.

22

It began to drizzle again as Edward stood and watched Armando DaSilva disappear into the manor house. Now would be the perfect time to spy on them but he would be seen if he tried to get to the twitten from his bedroom during the day. He would have to get there via the under-stairs cupboard.

He gave the man a few seconds before trying the main door but was almost seen by Albert who was making his way down the stairs. Edward heard an exchange of words between the two men as he held the door ajar.

He gave Albert half a minute to be out of sight before peering back into the hallway. The coast was clear and Edward stepped inside, closing the large door as quietly as he could.

He slinked across the parquet flooring to the staircase, listening and scanning for signs of anyone as he went. Distant murmurs from several directions were filtering into the hall. They were all reassuringly far away but it did not stop Edward's heart from racing with the thrill of being caught.

Before long, he was in the cupboard clambering over the boxes and suitcases to get to the sliding panel. It was tricky to find without his torch but he was soon crouching through the opening and into the void.

They were going to have words and Edward hated not being there to eavesdrop. DaSilva was steaming and was sure to say too much. In his eagerness to get to them, Edward had forgotten about the access hatch down into the cellar and had not given his eyes enough time to adjust.

As he clumsily fumbled for the metal ladder on the wall, disaster. He stepped through the hole and plummeted down into the abyss. During his descent he did manage to grab onto a rung but his weight and momentum forced him to let go and he hit the ground with a thud.

The cellar was pitch black and Edward's head was ringing. He had no idea if he had been unconscious or not, and if so, for how long. He knew he had just opened his eyes because he felt the movement of his lids but it was strange and disorienting to find he could still not see a thing.

The air was dank, thick with the smell of wet concrete and rotting wood. Edward got to his feet and was relieved to find he hadn't broken anything. Apart from the ringing in his ears and one of his thighs throbbing a little he felt fine. Clinging to the rung half way down had helped to slow his fall.

He scanned the eerie darkness as he felt for the ladder. A strange sense of being watched summoned a wave of goose bumps to creep across his skin. The sound of dripping water some distance away gave him an idea of the size of the subterranean room but the feeling of not being alone was overwhelming.

His imagination was obviously getting the better of him because he was convinced that someone was nearby. It was impossible to be sure but his senses were perceiving something in the pitch blackness. A presence, sinister or not, may have been giving off heat, breathing softly or creeping up on him. The moment Edward felt the ladder he bolted up it as fast as he could in the dark.

Before too long, the lad had reached the first floor level of the twitten and, with the light coming through the external vent, was finally able to see what he was doing.

With his heart racing he sat for a moment catching his breath as he looked down into the abyss, listening intensely. He had convinced himself that someone had been near him in the eerie darkness and was adamant to return soon with a flashlight.

As he recovered from his ordeal, he made his way to Sophia's room. He was hoping that they were still talking about him but found the room empty. Not wanting to give up, he crept along the twitten to DaSilva's room. His thigh was aching now and was beginning to stiffen up.

He found the man talking on the telephone as he sat at his dressing table. He was laughing and joking with someone in English and it sounded as though the conversation was about the contest.

As he stood and listened he felt his body shouting at him. His hand, the one he'd used to grab the ladder on his way down the cellar, was now stinging badly, his thigh was pounding and the ringing in his ears had been replaced by a sickening headache. He needed to get back to his room and lie down.

He gave the conversation a few more minutes before deciding to leave but then he heard DaSilva mention his name and he hobbled back to the vent.

"Yes," he said, as the person on the other end of the line was talking, "Yes, he's become a real problem but, eef your lad does his bit, eet all goes away."

DaSilva laughed at the person's reply and got to his feet as he prepared to hang up.

"Yes, but thees time will be different. Why? ahah, cuz the leetle shit deserves eet, that's why."

Edward had been right. One of Billingham's sons was going to pay him a visit, and by the sounds of it, a fatal one. DaSilva hung up and made his way to his bed still laughing.

"Unlike you, I don't keel innocent people," sneered the slimy man, repeating Edward's words from earlier, "You leetle fuck, neither do I.

He sat on the edge of the bed still smirking as he lit a cigarette.

"I get other's to do eet for me!" he added, chuckling.

That was how his dad was killed, thought Edward. Mr Billingham had pulled the trigger and not DaSilva as he had first assumed. It had been revenge for his brother's brain haemorrhage and, with DaSilva's help, he'd got away with it. That scenario made perfect sense which meant that his dad's murder may have had nothing to do with the secret surrounding Marie.

Edward limped back to the metal ladder. He daren't use the flat roof to get back to his room, the risk of being seen was too high. He had to go back the way he came, via the under-stairs cupboard.

Carefully, he negotiated the rungs and stepped off them into the ground floor enclosure. He then clambered through the cupboard and out into the hallway, checking that the coast was clear before emerging. He then slinked back across the hall and out through the main door.

Squinting through the light of day, he checked his wounds. The skin on his palm was grazed and had bled a little and his trousers were dirty around his thigh. He dusted himself down and made his way back to his room for further inspection.

23

His wounds consisted of nothing more than a few minor cuts and bruises and after a quick wash was almost as good as new. He made himself a bite to eat and waited in his room for Mr Carter's return.

As he ate his mind turned to the Billingham brother's. The contest would start on the Saturday morning sometime but that didn't mean they would pay him a visit that early. They could wait until later in the contest, sometime Sunday evening perhaps.

He gave it some thought as he looked across at the manor and came to the conclusion that he would be able to avoid them. He just needed to be vigilant. They were unlikely to come for him if someone else was in the barn and that left a fairly small window of opportunity, unless they were planning to come for him in the dead of night?

Edward shook his head, "Nah, too risky," he said, disagreeing with himself.

He tried to recall conversations he'd had with Dawson during the past week. He had told him more about the contest and what it meant for the staff of the manor house. Outside help was usually employed to cater for the influx of guests, more kitchen staff, cleaners and so on, which meant a lot of strange people milling around at all hours.

Sarah would be especially busy, as would Lisa,

and he may not see them a great deal. They would probably be too tired to hang around for long anyway. It would be possible for the brother's to come and go unseen he supposed, it just needed timing on their behalf.

Edward had the advantage. He knew they were coming and all he needed to do was keep on his toes. He could scramble out across the roof and onto the wall in under a minute, much faster than they could cross the courtyard and ascend the stairs. He felt confident he would evade them.

Mr Carter seemed to take an age to return and Edward had made himself several pots of tea before Lisa eventually came to collect him. Again, she was a sight for sore eyes and they chatted as they made their way through the manor house.

As they neared the dining room Lisa asked if he had the key.

"I was told to ask but I've only just remembered," she confessed.

Edward smiled and showed her the key just as Sophia and Mrs Simpson came down the stairs together. Edward felt that they'd been waiting for him because their timing was perfect. Mrs Carter had something to say.

Lisa was ushered away by her grandmother and Sophia escorted Edward through the dining room.

"Edward," she said, as they walked, "My husband is a very jealous man and if he hears talk of Marie not being his, there'll be violence."

She stopped and looked at the young man pleadingly, placing both her hands on his shoulders.

"I'm not saying she isn't," she added, making a point, "I'm saying rumours are dangerous, that's all, and William is waiting for a reason to......" she tapered off.

Edward looked into her eyes.

"A reason to, what?" he enquired.

Realising she looked as though she was begging she removed her hands from his shoulders and flicked back her hair, correcting her posture and regaining a little authority.

"Let's just say we're not getting along at the moment and a fantasy like yours would be the straw that broke the........." she was beginning to look flustered and upset, her eyes had welled up, "Any excuse and he'll......."

Edward stared at her unsympathetically.

"I'll keep my mouth shut," he agreed, "for now."

Mrs Carter wiped her eyes on a tissue she was conveniently holding before escorting Edward into the library. Her persona changed from whimpering damsel in distress to cold hearted bitch in a blink of an eye.

Edward felt she was playing him.

Mr Carter, Connor and DaSilva were standing around his desk as they entered and were discussing the strong box that had been placed in the centre.

"Have you bought the key, this time?" Mr Carter asked, scornfully, holding out his hand.

Begrudgingly, Edward gave it to him. He wanted to be the one who opened it but, for some reason, Mr Carter felt it was his right to do it for him. Why was he making such a fuss about it?

All eyes watched as he turned the key, released the latch and open the hinged lid. DaSilva tried to be the first to dive in but was stopped in his tracks by Mr Carter who gave him a stern look before scanning the items inside.

Edward saw the Portuguese scum bag glance directly at Sophia for a moment as her husband brushed him aside. With a raised brow he shook his head slightly as if giving her a sign. Whatever he was expecting to see wasn't there. Edward approached the desk as William began rifling through the contents.

He threw a handful of envelopes onto the desktop followed by a wad of loose sheets of paper, he then pulled out a small jewellery box and glanced at Edward briefly as he put it down. Edward was getting annoyed watching him delve through his parent's belongings.

"I am capable of looking through it myself, you know" he said, making a grab for the box, "I don't need any help."

He looked directly at DaSilva. "Or prying eyes," he added.

Mr Carter clung onto the box to prevent Edward from sliding it away and for a second or two they engaged in a mini tug of war.

"I'm curious why my wife asked Armando to retrieve it for her," he said, snatching the box from Edward's grasp and glaring at Sophia, "and why she hadn't come to me first, because there's nothing in here she'd want."

Embarrassed, Sophia smiled awkwardly as she thought of a reply.

"For Edward," she said, still thinking, "to make up for my behaviour towards him last week."

She stared at her husband and knew he had not believed her excuse.

"A mountain out of a mole hill, remember?" she asked, nodding.

Mr Carter slid his tongue across his teeth and clicked his lips as his stare remained fixed on his wife. Sophia had not lied to Edward about things being frosty between them because the man looked ready to explode.

Edward glanced at Connor and was surprised to see him looking back. The man raised one eyebrow in interest of the situation before returning his gaze back to Mr Carter. The tension between husband and wife was obvious and Edward relished it. Things were getting interesting.

"What were you expecting to find?" Mr Carter asked her, paying no attention to what she had said, and tapping the box, "and why would you think it was in here?"

Sophia flicked back her hair as her husband

slid the box towards her.

"Nothing," she replied, blushing slightly beneath her make-up, "I wasn't expecting anything."

Edward saw DaSilva tense up. He was clenching his teeth and his jaw muscles were dancing again. He was readying himself to defend her if necessary but, Connor had also read his body language and he took a step towards to him.

A shiver of excitement ran up Edward's back. It was strange witnessing the build up of hostility among the group and was glad to see that Mr Carter confronting Sophia. He was wishing for something violent to happen.

He knew that if he were to tell William about his suspicions now his wish would be realised. The man would slaughter the kissing cousins in a heartbeat but, what about Marie? The temptation to spill the beams was overwhelming but he bit his lip and simply enjoyed their awkward moment.

"So, you went behind my back to be kind to Edward?" William enquired, grimacing, "For nothing?"

Sophia, who was struggling for a reply, simply nodded.

"I don't believe you!"

Mr Carter sat down in his leather chair as he slid his hand inside his jacket. Slowly he produced a small blue diary and held it in the air. There were gold initials on the bottom corner. 'F.W.'

"Is this what you were looking for?" he asked,

stony faced.

Sophia's eyes widened ever so slightly but she did well to control her emotions. She pursed her lips and shook her head.

"It's not mine," she confessed.

Mr Carter looked up at DaSilva who also pursed his lips and shook his head, shrugging his shoulders for good measure.

Edward asked what it was.

"It was on top of the box with that newspaper," Mr Carter admitted, pointing briefly at the paper beneath the envelopes, "I'm not sure what it means but Gareth saw fit to hide it for some reason."

Sophia turned to leave but her husband told her to stay put.

"Don't you to want to look inside the box?" he barked, "but, you were so eager to have it bought here!"

"I did it for Edward!" she replied, still with her back to him.

"Then, what about the book?"

Sophia turned around stern faced. "What about it?" she snapped.

William flicked through the pages, stopping now and then to read it, as he worked his way to the last entry.

"It's a diary of sorts," explained Mr Carter, "But, not a personal one, more a job schedule with vague descriptions and no dates."

Sophia sniffed and flicked her hair back again. "So?"

"Seems the person was some sort of midwife, slash, abortionist."

Sophia sighed. "So?" she said again, getting agitated.

"Well, the last entry says 'S.C. The Manor House'," Mr Carter replied, "Any idea what that could mean?"

Sophia was struggling to remain calm and was turning the rings on her fingers round and around as her anxiety grew.

"No," she answered, with a nervous swallow, "I don't."

"You have no idea why your initials and our address have been written in an abortionist's diary?" Mr Carter snarled, "A diary my best friend hid under his pantry floor!"

Mr Carter was beginning to sound menacing, his face had reddened in anger and his nostrils were flaring. Sophia shook her head meekly, she was clearly afraid of him.

DaSilva begun to explain that there must be a hundred stately homes in the area and the note in the diary could mean any one of them but Mr Carter shouted him down.

"I'm not interested in your opinion," he snapped, his eyes never leaving his wife, "Answer me!" he demanded.

Sophia's eyes were now welled with tears. Edward was engrossed in her agony and the hairs on his arms were standing on end.

"William. I have no idea," she sobbed, "It isn't

me!"

Mr Carter slammed the diary down onto the desk.

"I don't believe you!" he growled.

"Surely you don't think I've been unfaithful to you?"

"What do you think?"

Sophia acted shocked, "William!" she gasped, "No, never!"

Mr Carter turned to Edward and asked him if he knew anything about the diary or if Gareth had ever mentioned Sophia. The lad shook his head. He was clearly thinking his dad had slept with her and that she had aborted his child at some point.

"But you know something's going on, don't you?" William goaded, "These two have been acting weird ever since you arrived."

DaSilva objected.

"And I've had enough!" he snarled, glaring at his wife's cousin.

Mr Carter threw the diary into the strong box and replaced the newspaper, envelopes and the jewellery. He then closed the lid.

"I want the truth or I'm going to lose my temper," he said, eventually, through gritted teeth.

"The boy's been snooping around," confessed DaSilva, "that's why I've been acting a beet odd. Sophia too."

"No," William said, sitting down, "Your behaviour changed the moment I told you he would be staying here. The whispering, the sly looks between you, had already started."

Again, DaSilva objected.

"Explain the diary," demanded Mr Carter abruptly, glaring at his wife.

Sophia stepped forward. "I can't," she said, her mouth quivering pitifully, "I have no idea what it means."

"Isn't it obvious what it means?" William snapped, "You've had an abortion!"

Sophia began to sob. "No. William. I haven't, I swear!" she snivelled, "and I've always been faithful to you."

Edward huffed to himself quietly. He was impressed at her acting skills.

Mr Carter looked at DaSilva.

"I want you gone after the contest," he said, looking back at his wife, "You've out stayed your welcome."

Edward was expecting DaSilva to protest and create a scene but the slimy man simply glared down at Mr Carter. His eyes narrowed menacingly as he clenched his teeth in anger. Connor poised himself for a confrontation.

"What about the boy?" Armando snarled, contemptuously, "Does he go too?"

William glanced at Edward for a moment and looked him up and down as he gave it some thought. DaSilva seemed anxious about him staying for some reason. What was he afraid of?

"He stays," he replied, glaring back at his cousin-in law, "for now."

The Portuguese hit man diverted his menacing glare to Edward and they stared at each other intensely for a moment. Edward gave the man a smug grin before looking away.

"What about me?" Sophia enquired, looking pitiful, "Am I going?"

William sighed deeply as he sat back heavily in his leather chair. His eyes were red and he was clearly upset. To him she had committed the ultimate betrayal and then had the evidence ripped from her body.

"I don't know," he said, calming down a little, "I just want everyone to act normal for this weekend and I'll decide afterwards."

"Thees is bullsheet!" snarled DaSilva, "I get sent home like some naughty keed for what? Some fuckeen book?"

Mr Carter shot to his feet and lunged towards Armando, grabbing a fistful of his pullover. The man went to retaliate but thought again as Connor stepped in.

"No," growled Mr Carter, forcing DaSilva backwards a little, "because I don't fucking like you."

Sophia gasped. "William!" she snapped, genuinely surprised at his confession.

"I never have!" William continued, drowning her out.

DaSilva also looked shocked to learn the truth but remained silent.

"And I've put up with you long enough!"

William added.

Armando steadied himself on his feet before forcing William's hand from his jumper. The two men glared at each other as DaSilva unruffled himself.

"The feeling ees mutual!" he snarled, "Bautista's not going to like thees."

William huffed smugly. "I don't give a shit if he likes it or not,"

Bautista, Sophia's brother, had gone with friends to a matinee in town and Mr Carter asked her if he had returned yet. She shook her head but kept her mouth shut.

"We'll tell him together if you like," William sneered, "as soon as he returns."

DaSilva glowered at Mr Carter for a few moments as if thinking of a response but suddenly turned around and stormed out of the room

24

Edward watched DaSilva leave. He could not believe that Mr Carter had just banished him before his eyes, sent him packing. There was no saying what DaSilva's next move would be but Edward sensed that things were about to get ugly.

Mr Carter thanked Connor for sticking around but said that he could leave and go home if he liked and, after a little persuading, he did, winking at Edward as he passed him by.

The boy now found himself alone with the feuding husband and wife. Sophia, who had also watched DaSilva leave, turned to her husband.

"This is madness, William," she said, sorrowfully, "You're willing to destroy everything because of a coincidence?"

"You mean, an abortionists diary with your initials in it? Yes!"

"But, I've never been unfaithful," she said, glancing at Edward slyly, "and I've never had an abortion!"

William glared at her angrily for a moment before looking at Edward. He had spotted the brief glance she had made and sensed that Edward could tell him more.

"What's going on, Edward?" he asked, sternly, "Tell me!"

Edward looked at Sophia. She was wide eyed

and tense lipped as she held her breath. She looked terrified that he was about to reveal everything and that her world would be ruined.

There was no need to pretend any more, the man knew that something was going on between his wife and her cousin and that they were hiding a secret worth lying for. Edward struggled with knowing where to begin.

"She has my mom's jewellery," he said, still looking into her eyes, "things she was wearing the day she went missing."

Puzzled, William frowned and looked at his wife.

"And, I think DaSilva had her killed and then my dad," he continued.

Edward had been thinking about the gold letters on the diary Mr Carter had found. He had not made the connection at first, he knew it was a clue but, it hadn't dawned on him until now what it was.

Mr Carter asked Sophia why she had Heather's jewellery but she refused to answer. Edward revealed his theory.

"I think the diary belongs to Charles Walker's wife," he said, "The man DaSilva blamed for shooting my dad."

William now looked bewildered. Being kept in the dark until now he had no idea how complex this whole thing was. He had sensed that Sophia had been hiding something from him, an abortion or termination, and that DaSilva had helped her but, murder?

Sophia was shocked that Edward had revealed so much. Tears had begun to trickle down her face and she looked at him as if he had just tore her heart out. Her eyes were pleading with him not to mention Marie.

"I'm not exactly sure what really happened," he confessed, "but it's all connected somehow."

"Sophia?" William demanded, "What the hell have you done?"

Flustered, she looked at her husband and then back at Edward. She began to cry and ran from the room hysterically, slamming the door behind her. The truth had not quite come out but her behaviour definitely pointed the finger of guilt in her direction, guilty of what was still to be determined.

Mr Carter was perplexed and he sat down again scratching his head. He was struggling to make sense of it all, struggling to believe it as he stared at the strong box.

"I regret ever bringing you here, Edward," he said, his eyes never leaving it, "and I curse the day you arrived."

Edward could sense the man's anger turning on him, a scapegoat he could blame for his life turning to shit. That wasn't going to happen.

"I didn't want to come here," said the lad, angrily, "and I'm not the one who's ruined your life. They are!"

Mr Carter averted his gaze to him briefly.

"And don't forget, I'm a victim too," Edward added, prodding himself.

There was an awkward silence as Edward waited for Mr Carter to respond but the man just sat back in his office chair and said nothing.

"My parents are dead because of them,"

William remained still. His eyes had almost glazed over in a frozen stare. He was still trying to piece things together in his mind but refused to accept his wife was a murderer.

"Mr Billingham may have pulled the trigger but it was Armando who orchestrated it."

The name Billingham jolted Mr Carter back to life. Confused, he glared at the lad with a furrowed brow.

"Revenge for my dad giving his brother brain damage," Edward explained, nodding knowingly.

William suddenly got angry and slammed both hands onto the desk as he rose from his chair. The story was becoming more and more unbelievable.

"For god's sake, Edward!" he bawled, "Who you going to accuse next in this fucking fantasy of yours?"

"Fantasy?" Edward repeated, confused, "Why does everyone keep saying that? It's no fantasy!"

"Yes, it is!"

William grabbed the strong box from the desk and stomped around to the lad, thrusting it into his arms aggressively.

"Get out of my sight!" he growled.

"But, it's true," Edward snapped, "I haven't made it up!"

Mr Carter grabbed his arm and spun him around and then proceeded to frog march him towards the door.

"It's all connected somehow!" Edward explained, desperate for the man to believe him, "And, I think Marie has something to do with it!"

Mr Carter stopped in his tracks, jolting Edward backwards violently and causing him to drop the strong box, spilling its contents. He spun the lad around again and grabbed him by his throat, forcing him up against the door.

"What?" William snarled, his eyes filled with pure rage.

Shocked by the speed the man had manoeuvred him into a strangle hold, Edward struggled for a few moments to answer. Mr Carter shook him angrily and repeated the question.

"My dad found out something," choked Edward, " and DaSilva got Billingham to kill him."

Edward still felt reluctant to reveal what he really thought because he would be putting Marie in danger. Mr Carter's grip tightened.

"He then lied about it to cover for him!" gasped the lad.

"What did he find out?" snarled Mr Carter, red faced and fuming.

"I don't know!"

Sighing loudly, and without warning, William flung the lad violently to the ground, sending him sprawling on all fours through the items from the strong box.

"I'm sick of half truths!" he ranted, "and only getting part of the story!"

Edward scrambled back to his feet as Mr Carter lunged towards him. The lad scarpered back towards the desk and managed to evade capture by keeping it between them.

"I don't know what he found out," Edward explained, "but, whatever it was, my dad was murdered for it."

Mr Carter angrily marched back and forth around the desk in a futile attempt to catch young Edward. In frustration, he threw a few desktop items at him to force a mistake or error in judgement, but the lad was too quick and avoided each missile.

"So, you don't even know for sure that Marie is involved?" he sneered, hurling a note pad at the lad, "You've simply assumed?"

"I didn't say involved," Edward clarified, "just that it may have something to do with her."

By now, William was out of breath and he slumped down in his chair as Edward stood in front of the desk.

"Your wife is hiding something and her cousin has killed to protect it," added Edward, relaxing a little now the chase was over, "I've tried to find out what exactly but, can't quite get to the truth."

"You've jumped to conclusions," Mr Carter puffed, "I agree that she's hiding something from me but, murder? No!"

"Then, how has she got my mom's jewellery?" Edward asked, highlighting a fact he was sure of.

Mr Carter sat and stared at him without reply. His expression was one of bemusement, he was thinking it over but could not answer him.

"Jewellery that should have burned in the fire?" added the lad.

William pursed his lips and shook his head a little, he went to speak but stopped himself as he gave it more thought.

"And why was my dad killed seven years later along with the husband of the woman who owns that ....?" he was about to say book but was interrupted.

"Stop!" Mr Carter bawled, "There's no proof that Mr Walker's related to F.W. Just because the last initial's the same means nothing. You've jumped to conclusions!"

Edward shook his head defiantly.

"You've put two and two together and made five!" added William.

"No," Edward remarked, "It's all connected and you know it!"

Mr Carter closed his eyes, sighing deeply. He began to take even breaths as he tried to calm himself a little. The unfolding drama had upset him and he was confused on how to handle it.

"I bet they're up there now concocting some lie to tell you," Edward said, beginning to collect the items from the box. "They're always whispering together."

William knew that there had to be a logical answer to it all. Edward was jumping to conclusions and confusing everyone by going from one accusation to another. His wife had terminated an unwanted pregnancy, that was all, she was not responsible for killing anyone.

Having Heather's jewellery was a question that needed answering, and he could understand why the lad's imagination was running wild about it, but he could not see a connection between that and the book.

"Look!" William puffed, eventually, "I can buy the story of Billingham pulling the trigger, and even Armando covering it up, but your mom's death was a tragic accident and the two are totally unrelated."

"Believe what you want," said Edward, still occupied with the scattered contents of his father's strong box, "But mark my words. Once I prove that bastard murdered my parents I'm going to kill him, and anyone else involved."

Edward had almost refilled the box with his belongings but froze as he picked up the newspaper. He was about to simply toss it away before noticing the date, 22nd of August 1954, the day after the fire.

25

There had to be a reason why his dad had kept the newspaper and Edward quickly scanned through the first few pages. He had assumed it would have an article about the fire and he was right but, there was something else.

There was another item of news circled in red pen directly below the story of how the fire had killed two women. It was about a another woman that had gone missing at the same time as his mother. Edward read a snippet of the article out loud.

"And while one of the missing women died in the above mentioned fire the fate of the second, a Mrs Fiona Walker, remains unknown. Mrs Walker, a respected midwife, went missing on the same day as Heather Kane, one of the victims of the aforementioned blaze, and the two were originally thought to be connected........."

Edward looked at Mr Carter who was looking back at him.

"I was right," he said, walking over to the desk and throwing the paper across it, "F.W. Is Walker's wife."

William grabbed the paper and read the article.

"She went missing the same time as my mom," added Edward, "How's that for a coincidence?"

Mr Carter stared at the paper for a while as he digested what it could mean and Edward told him that this must be what his dad had discovered and why DaSilva had him killed.

"The murders are connected," he remarked, "and that bastard's guilty of both."

Mr Carter held up a hand to stop Edward's ranting.

"Hold on," he snapped, "I don't see a connection."

Edward was flabbergasted. How did the man not see it?

"My mom died seven years ago," he explained, "Your wife has her jewellery. My dad finds, or is given, that diary and newspaper and then confronts DaSilva about it who has him killed by making Billingham think he's doing him a favour."

"But, how would Gareth know DaSilva had anything to do with it?" enquired Mr Carter, throwing the paper back onto the desk, "This article points no fingers, and it even states the incidences are unrelated."

Edward had already thought of that himself and the answer was blatantly obvious.

"Charles Walker," he said, confidently.

William was about to refute him but stopped as the penny dropped.

"It makes sense, I suppose," he said, nodding in agreement.

There was no denying it, the connection was there.

"And he must have found the diary and then told your dad." added William.

Edward felt strangely relieved that he had managed to link his parents deaths together and for someone else to finally believe him. However, although the connection was established, the motive for the fire remained unknown. The reason for his dad's murder was clear but why have his mom killed? He aired his query to Mr Carter.

"And I don't see how it has anything to do with Marie?" William remarked, airing his own thoughts, "What made you think that?"

Edward shrugged.

"Just a feeling I suppose," he replied, wishing he had never mentioned her name, "Vibes I got from Sophia and him."

"Vibes?"

"Yes, you know? The way they reacted when her name was mentioned and the looks between them if questioned."

"Questioned?"

Edward sighed. He had to get Mr Carter's mind off Marie because if he found out she was someone else's daughter there was no telling what he would do.

"Now that we have a connection between mom and dad, and the whole thing's a bit clearer, I think I was jumping to conclusions about Marie," he lied, faking sincerity.

Mr Carter glared at him for a while as he examined his expression, looking for even the smallest sign of deceit but, Edward was too good an actor and fooled him into believing his explanation.

"So," William said, eventually, "The question is, why get rid of Heather?"

Just then, and as if on cue, there was a short rap on the door and in walked Mrs Simpson. A sly, miserable, woman who reminded Edward of an old vulture with her long curved nose and down turned mouth.

"A word if I may, Mr Carter," she said, glaring at Edward, "In private."

Mr Carter asked the lad to wait outside in the dining room and not to go away. He was eager to continue their discussion. Edward left the room and could feel the old hags eyes burning into the back of his head.

As soon as he closed the door he pressed his ear up against it in the hope of eavesdropping but, apart from an inaudible drone, nothing distinctive could be heard.

Five minutes dragged by and Edward was getting bored. The kissing cousins were upstairs somewhere preparing their story to tell Mr Carter and he was itching to go and listen to them.

They had no idea that a connection between his parents murders had been made and was interested how they would explain it. He smiled to himself as he imagined their faces when confronted with the facts.

Just then the door to the library opened and Mr

Carter called him in. Mrs Simpson was sat in front of the desk and Mr Carter asked the lad to take a seat beside her. The man had pity written across his face as he sat down.

"Mrs Simpson has shed new light on the matter," William informed him, "She says that Sophia did call for the midwife but, not for herself for your mother."

 The lad was stunned.

"Edward. It was she who had the termination, not my wife."

Edward shook his head in denial.

"You lying bitch!" he snarled, jumping to his feet and glaring at the old hag, "You're just saying what they want you to say!"

The two had concocted an excuse quicker than he had anticipated.

"I beg your pardon!" exclaimed Mrs Simpson, shocked by the boys outburst.

"You heard me!" he snarled, "you lying bitch!"

"Edward!" snapped Mr Carter, "Calm yourself!"

"But, this is bollocks. She's helping them!"

"Just calm down and listen,"

Edward grabbed the paper from off the desk and waved it at Mr Carter.

"We know what happened, we've just made the connection!"

"Yes I know, but if you let me explain, you'll see that the connection is the same!"

"How can it be, she's lying?"

"Listen you wretched boy!" bellowed Mrs

Simpson, "shut your mouth and listen to what Mr Carter has to say!"

"Why should I, he'll only be repeating your lies?"

"Just because you don't want to hear something doesn't make it a lie!" she snapped, "Sometimes the truth hurts!"

"It's a lie, why would my mom have an abortion?"

"There were complications!" William replied, "She had no choice. She came here for help, stayed the night with the midwife and they left together the next morning."

"And you didn't notice?"

"I must have been away on business at the time."

"How convenient."

"Heather went to her great aunts house and Mrs Walker....well....err...."

"Disappeared?"

William shrugged, "Yes I suppose, but god knows where she went next or who she met. I'd expect that, in her profession, she'd been to some right hovels full of shifty characters, anything could've happened."

"I don't believe you're buying this!" Edward snarled, "It's not true!"

"As god is my witness," Mrs Simpson, piped up, "I let her in myself and saw them both leave the next morning, I am not lying!"

"Think about it, Edward," Mr Carter said, trying

to make the boy see sense, "It explains everything."

"No, it doesn't," snapped the lad, "Why does Sophia have her jewellery, why was dad murdered by the abortionists husband?"

"The jewellery was left here unknowingly," replied Mrs Simpson, "Mrs Carter was going to return it to her but she died in that terrible fire."

"And Charles Walker must've found the diary years later and somehow blame Gareth for her disappearance," Mr Carter added.

Edward frowned at the logic.

"He blamed my dad after seeing the words 'S,C The Manor House' scrawled in a diary?" Edward snarled, "Do me a favour!"

William got to his feet and walked around to the boy. He could feel his pain, the lad wanted closure and needed to have someone to blame so that he could avenge their deaths. He was unable to grasp, or accept, the truth.

"I admit that there are still questions that need answers," he said, as he neared Edward, "but, as far as I'm concerned, I believe Mrs Simpson's explanation. It fits and there's no reason she would lie."

"You believe it because it's manufactured for you, it takes the blame and focus off Sophia, and she's lying to protect them!"

"It makes more sense than the fantasy you almost had me fooled with!"

Edward growled with anger and rattled the newspaper in frustration. A moment ago the man was on the same page as him, they were going to solve the mystery together, and now some old hag had convinced him otherwise. He was so frustrated that tears were welling in his eyes again.

"So now I bet you think DaSilva's innocent too?" he snarled.

"I see now reason why not!"

"Fuck! I don't believe this"

"Like Mrs Simpson said, the truth is hard to accept, " William offered, walking up to the lad and placing his hands onto his shoulders, "and you're trying so hard to avenge your parents that you're creating an enemy to blame. For you DaSilva's guilty and you can't accept anything else."

Edward shrugged Mr Carter's hands free of his shoulders and took several steps backwards.

"If Walker killed my dad at his own house," Edward snarled through gritted teeth, "then how did the diary end up under my pantry floor?"

William pursed his lips and shook his head slightly as the lad stepped up to the desk and grabbed the little blue book.

"I don't know," he replied, "That's one of many questions that we'll probably never know the answer to. The people involved are dead."

Edward felt the tears run down his cheeks and he turned around to wipe them away with his sleeve. He spotted the strong box on the floor and made his way towards it. He had heard enough. Somehow the incestuous cousins had turned the tables on him and there would be no convincing

Mr Carter to the contrary. In his eyes the matter had been resolved.

"When I asked Sophia about the jewellery she said that she'd borrowed it," snivelled Edward, stuffing the paper and diary into the box before picking it up, "Why lie when she could've just said what you just have?"

"She probably didn't want to upset you with the truth," replied Mrs Simpson, pausing briefly before offering her view, "She was protecting you."

The old bag was going to have an answer for everything, they had coaxed her well. Dare he mention Marie not being Mr Carter's daughter?

"So, why has Armando arranged for the Billingham brothers to kill me if there's nothing to hide?" Edward queried, turning to face them as he reached the door.

William scoffed as he and Mrs Simpson looked at each other briefly. It was obvious that they did not believe him.

"Nonsense!" retorted William, "You're mistaken, or ill informed."

"I heard him on the telephone, myself."

"Then you've probably got the wrong end of the stick. Why on earth would DaSilva want you dead?"

Edward opened the library door.

"Good question," he replied, looking out across the dining room, "Let's go and ask him."

Mr Carter gave a deep tired sigh. He was satisfied that the issue had been resolved and was growing weary of the accusations. He told Edward to return to his room and accept what Mrs Simpson had said as the truth of the matter.

"I don't want to hear anymore about it," he said as Edward turned to leave, "Is that clear?"

26

Edward made his way back through the dining room and into the hallway. The interfering old cow had done her job well and he had to admit that if he were Mr Carter he would probably believe her too. It did make some sense.

Mr Carter had originally believed his wife was an adulterer who had terminated a pregnancy, and at one point had been told she was a murderer, he was obviously going to believe Mrs Simpson's lie about her being a good Samaritan who tried to hide a secret.

However, Edward knew differently. He had witnessed her behaviour and heard her conversations with DaSilva. Mrs Simpson's story had gaping holes in it that Mr Carter would rather leave unanswered, After all, if Edward's version was true his wife would be responsible for at least two deaths.

He closed the dining room door behind him and stood in the hallway. The box was getting heavy but he had no intention of going back to the barn via the kitchen, the likelihood of answering questions was too high.

Before making his way over to the main door he happened to glance up at the atrium and was surprised to see Armando grinning back down at him as he leant against the balustrade.

The two adversaries glared at each other for a while without blinking but as Mr Carter and Mrs Simpson emerged from the dining room, Armando slinked away.

"Why are you still here?" boomed Mr Carter, closing the door, "You should be back in your room by now, surely."

Edward, who was still glaring up at the atrium with his back to Mr Carter, told him that DaSilva had kept him back for a staring contest.

"But, now he's chickened out, I'll leave." he added.

At that point, Albert, appeared from the corridor that led to the kitchen and Mr Carter asked him to escort young Edward back to the barn.

"Oh, and Edward," William said, as the lad began to follow the old man, "Remember, this matter is now resolved and I expect your shenanigans to end, I hope I'm making myself clear?"

Edward did not reply or make any effort to show that he had heard Mr Carter. As long as his wife appeared squeaky clean the man was happy with the story the old bag had fed him but Edward knew it had been a clever, fabricated, lie. He left the hall thinking of his next move.

Albert never uttered a single word as they made their way to the kitchen and he disappeared as soon as he had ushered the lad into the room, closing the door quickly behind himself.

He was acting odd, almost sheepish in fact, and Edward felt that the old man was deliberately avoiding eye contact with him. Walking with his face turned away at all times and anxious to get rid of him. He had looked ashamed of himself or guilty of something but, guilty of what?

Sarah greeted Edward with a smile and, although she already suspected what the box was, she asked what he was carrying. She could tell that he had been crying from the redness of his eyes but said nothing about it.

"It looks heavy," she added, clearing a spot on the table for him to put it down for a moment.

Edward complied with a huff of relief.

"It's just some of my mom's things," he informed her, "You know, from home? Mr Carter got them for me."

Sarah nodded, saying she was glad it had been sorted out so quickly for him and Edward thanked her for asking about it in the first place.

He spent a few minutes explaining what was inside but was anxious to get back to his room and Sarah eventually let him go with a hot pork sandwich wrapped in paper and balanced on top of the box.

He made himself a pot of tea and ate the snack at the kitchen bench as he thought about DaSilva grinning down at him from the atrium. If the issue had been resolved and the old bag's account of events had been true, then why would the scum bag still be acting suspiciously?

Surely, if there was nothing left to hide then there was no need to keep playing him or trying to provoke a response. He obviously enjoyed their little feud and his smile wasn't saying *"See, I told you I was innocent"* it was saying, *"It's your move!"*

They were a pair of slippery eels and able to wriggle their way out of anything he could throw at them. They were clever and cunning with years of lying and manipulating experience, compared to them Edward was a novice.

It then occurred to the lad that, unlike him, they still had everything to lose. His life had already been turned upside down and there was nothing more anyone could do to him.

He liked the children's home and if being sent back there was the worst they could do then he may as well make his next move a decisive one. Drastic action was called for and DaSilva was in for a shock.

Albert's persona earlier was also vexing him. The old man was usually such a proud individual that demanded respect but he was far from that when he had led Edward to the kitchen. Why had he acted so odd?

It was just getting dark as he climbed out onto the roof. He had decided that there was no point in waiting for everyone to go to bed because he was going to risk everything to get to the truth and he didn't care who witnessed it. If this was to be his last day here, then so be it.

He jogged along the wall and then tiptoed across the flat roof. He peered down through the lantern and was glad to see that DaSilva was there. He was sat on a sofa with Bautista, Sophia's brother, deep in conversation.

The women were nowhere in sight but Mr Carter was setting up the snooker table ready for a game. Edward wondered if he and DaSilva had made up or were just putting on a show for his brother-in-law.

Not wanting to hang around too long, Edward climbed through the vent, replaced the slats, and made his way along the narrow twitten directly to Armando's room. He unclipped the vent and lowered it onto the carpet, along with his rucksack, before clambering out of the hidden passage.

His heart was racing. He could not believe that he was actually going through with his insane plan. There would be no going back from it and the outcome was far from predictable but, they had left him no other choice.

He grabbed a flat wooden gun box from beneath DaSilva's bed and opened the lid as he placed in onto the mattress. The pistol came equipped with extra magazines, loose bullets and a silencer all held in place by a velvet padded inlay with cut-outs for each. He stuffed them into his rucksack and slid it back onto his shoulder.

On the underside of the lid were basic

illustrated instructions on how to load and unload the weapon and before long Edward was armed and ready. He practiced aiming at random objects around the room as he waited for his prey and he tried out different hiding places that gave him the best vantage point.

The longer he held the weapon the calmer he became and the more he thought about his actions the more sense they made. It was the only way he was going to get that bastard to tell the truth and he was willing to put a bullet in him if necessary.

After trying several positions around the room Edward decided on his first choice, behind the door. It was the only place he could block an escape if the man tried to run. The confrontation would happen sooner but that could not be helped.

He opened the door slightly and peered down the corridor. He was getting restless and eager to get his plan in motion. He could hear voices off in the distance, Lisa giggling mixed with a mans dulcet tone.

Sophia's door at the far end of the other wing was ajar and Edward could see the light escaping through it. He could hear Marie and knew she was in there too. He savoured the peacefulness of the moment, knowing full well that, very soon, life in 'The Manor House' would change forever.

They had driven him to this act and he was here because of them. Their secret was coming out one way or the other and Edward was not going to stop until he had the truth, no matter who got hurt in the process.

A few hours went by but, at last, Edward heard DaSilva speaking to someone as he made his way towards his room. He was telling them he would be back shortly for a re-match and needed to get more cigarettes.

The lad readied himself with the pistol. He had begun to have second thoughts but it was now too late to back down. He forced himself against the wall and waited anxiously for the face off.

Armando switched on the light as he entered the room and then closed the door behind himself with the tips of his fingers without looking back. Edward's presence had gone unnoticed and he quickly turned the key in the lock, trapping his prey inside.

27

DaSilva turned as the lock clicked into place and was shocked to see Edward standing there, armed and ready to shoot him.

"What the fuck are you doing?" he gasped, "Are you eesane?"

Edward stepped away from the door and into the light.

"I want the truth," he snarled.

DaSilva quickly glanced around for something he could use as a weapon but was too far away from anything useful. He began to back off.

"But, you know the truth," he said, nearing the dressing table, "Meesis Simpson told you."

Edward ordered the man to stand still but was forced to fire a warning shot at the dressing table. He was glad he had opted to fit the silencer but the gunshot was still quite loud. Bits of wood splintered into the air as the bullet hit and DaSilva stopped dead. He knew the lad meant business.

"That was bullshit, and you know it." Edward said, through gritted teeth, "You're going to tell me what really happened or I'll.......".

The gun trembled wildly in his hand and DaSilva knew the lad was nervous. He quickly weighed up the odds of being able to jump him before the trigger was pulled but decided against it. The lad despised him and would fire the moment he made his move.

"A man weel confess to anytheen weeth a gun in his face." offered DaSilva, slyly, "I weel say anything you want me to."

"As long as it's the truth."

"How weel you know?"

Edward smiled and waved the gun towards the telephone that sat on the dressing table covered in bits of wood.

"Call Billingham," he ordered, calmly, "tell him you need to talk urgently."

DaSilva frowned and asked why.

"Just get him here!" replied Edward sternly.

The man picked up the telephone receiver and began to dial a number.

"Keep it brief and say you need to see him in person," Edward instructed, "Deviate or warn him in any way and I will shoot you."

DaSilva did as he was told and managed to convince Mr Billingham to come to the manor under the pretence of having urgent information too sensitive to be spoken over the telephone.

With phase one of his plan complete, Edward unlocked the door and peered down the corridor. Sophia's bedroom door was still ajar and he told DaSilva to head straight for it.

"I don't have a problem with shooting you in the back," he warned the slimy man as they walked, "So don't try anything stupid."

He kept a decent distance between himself and DaSilva. The guy could not be trusted and if he were to try something Edward needed space to react. He was struggling to hold his nerve. His heart was beating through his ribs and his hand was getting sweaty. He followed Armando into Mrs Carter's room.

She was sat at her dressing table filing her nails but jumped to her feet in surprise as they entered. Mrs Simpson was also there and was putting items of clothing back into one of the wardrobes, she too was shocked to see Edward with a pistol. She closed the wardrobe and stepped over to Sophia.

Mrs Carter gawped at Armando with pleading eyes but neither woman said a word until Edward asked where Marie was. The girl was nowhere to be seen.

"I've just put her to bed." replied Mrs Simpson, sneeringly.

"Which room?"

"First on the left."

Edward glared at Sophia. "And your sister in-law," he asked, "What room is she in?"

"At the end of the corridor," she replied, contemptuously, "also on the left."

He ordered everyone from the bedroom and told Mrs Simpson to lock Marie's door before ushering them to the end of the corridor.

Although she had been relieved that her daughter had been kept out of it, Sophia could not hold her tongue any longer and asked Edward if he had lost his mind. "How on earth do you think this will end?"

The lad ignored her and told DaSilva to open Bautista's door. He did as he was told and then stepped aside. The faint voice of the thin woman was heard asking who was there and Sophia entered the room. She spoke in Portuguese for a few seconds before stepping back out and locking the door.

"She's not very well," she snapped, leaving the key in the lock, "and I want her out of harms way if you don't mind."

Edward had not wanted the women locked up but having one less hostage to handle made sense. He knew that she had no telephone in her room and the chances of her trying to escape through the window were very low and so he agreed, ordering everyone else down the stairs.

His initial anxiety had now settled and his confidence was growing. The gun made him feel powerful and in complete control of the situation but could not let himself get carried away. He needed to stay alert and ready for any potential attack.

The large grandfather clock struck seven and began to chime as they descended down into the hallway. Edward told them to head for the dining room but they all stopped dead half way down the lower flight as Sarah appeared from the kitchen corridor carrying a tray of sandwich triangles.

It took her a few seconds to realise what was going on.

"Edward!" She gasped, "have you lost your

mind?"

Sophia huffed and told her she had said the same thing only a few moments ago. "God knows what he hopes to accomplish," she added.

The lad remained calm as he eyed the tray.

"I thought dinner had finished hours ago," he remarked.

Sarah looked blankly at the group for a few moments until realising that Edward was referring to the tray of food.

"Oh. it's just light refreshments to break the evening." she informed him, "They'll all be along shortly."

"Perfect!"

Edward told everyone to make their way into the dining room, told them where to sit, to not make a sound or doing anything that would warn the others. They did as they were instructed and the lad closed the door behind them, leaving it slightly ajar for a view of the hallway.

Before long, the sound of clinking glasses and mumbling voices could be heard coming from the snooker room corridor and Edward readied himself to confront the group. Timing his exit he stepped from the dining room and quickly made his way out across the hallway.

Surprised, the trio instantly stopped talking as they saw Edward with the pistol and he ordered them into the dining room. Mr Carter was furious and angrily strode towards the lad but stopped as the headlights of a car flashed across the hallway briefly as it pulled up outside.

"That'll be Billingham," explained Edward, watching Mr Carter's expression change from anger to puzzlement and then back to anger.

Edward shouted down the man's furious questions and ordered him to take the tray of drinks from Albert so that he could answer the door. Bautista had already slinked inside the dining room out of harms way.

Fuming, but perplexed, William eventually signalled to the old man to do as Edward had demanded and, with a warning from Edward not to cause suspicion, Albert waited for the door bell to ring.

Mr Carter was ushered into the room and Edward stood across the threshold trying to keep his eyes on all his hostages at the same time. Everyone had remained seated and Mr Carter approached the table, put down the tray and sat next to Sophia.

Mr Billingham entered the huge hallway and took off his overcoat, handing it to Albert , it was then he spotted the boy and his mouth dropped. The car he had arrived in could be heard driving away from the house and any chance of escape along with it.

"Albert?" he questioned, suspiciously.

"This way sir, if you please," the old man said, solemnly.

Edward stepped aside to let the two men through the doorway, training the pistol at Mr

Billingham's torso. The large bearded man glared at him as he passed, his eyes filled with hatred. Edward grimaced back at him, this man had killed his dad and he was going to pay for it this very night.

Just then, Lisa suddenly appeared at his side making Edward jump a little and almost pull the trigger.

"What's going on?" She asked, before spotting the pistol and then everyone else sat around the table. She gasped as the penny dropped.

Edward did his best to calm her and tried to explain what he was doing but she began to step away from him shocked and scared.

"I promise this will all make sense but I need you to trust me!" He pleaded, "I need your help with this, please!"

Lisa, the colour drained from her face, stood looking at the lad, at the gun and at the group of hostages. Her Nan and grandfather were sat looking back at her.

"Please," Edward repeated, "If it goes to plan it'll be over before you know it."

Struggling to show a brave face she asked how she could help him.

"Anything to end this!" She added.

Edward leant towards her and whispered as he clasped her hand in his.

"Trust me, Lisa, please!"

They stared at each other for a moment as she wiped a nervous tear from her cheek but, eventually, she managed a half smile and asked again what she could do for him.

"I need you to fetch Dawson, Stefan and Mrs Holland here, purely as witnesses of course," he explained, "I don't want anyone free to call the police just yet, not until this is over. Do you understand?"

Lisa nodded, wiping her cheek again.

"Tell them that there's a staff meeting about the contest or something but keep calm and don't get them suspicious. Ok?"

Again, the young women nodded.

"This is madness," she said, still staring at him, "and there'll be no going back after this!"

"I know, but I've no other choice and I've gone too far to give up now."

Lisa promised she'd try her best and glanced towards her grandparents briefly before leaving across the hall.

Edward turned to face his captives.

28

Edward left the door ajar and asked everyone to be remain seated and to put their hands on the table top in plain sight. While everyone complied, Mr Billingham protested. He had been giving DaSilva daggers ever since he'd sat down.

"Why am I here?" he shouted angrily still glaring at DaSilva, "What the fuck's been said?"

DaSilva shrugged but said nothing.

"If this is a set up!" he snarled menacingly, getting to his feet "I swear I'll...............!"

"Just sit down and shut up!" shouted Edward, pointing the pistol at him, "Whatever you have to say will have to wait for the others."

"William!" Billingham snarled, "Is this your doing?"

"No," replied Edward, smugly, "It's mine."

Billingham glared back at DaSilva before sitting down and placing his hands on the table cloth. It was obvious the man knew why he was there and Edward was glad he was already blaming DaSilva for it.

Soon enough, voices could be heard approaching the room and the lad positioned himself beside the door as he waited for them to enter. Mrs Holland was first to appear followed by Dawson, Stefan and then Lisa. Edward had already taken a few steps further away just in case one of the men had the thought to jump him.

They all fell silent and looked around questioningly. Edward quickly explained the situation to them before asking them to take a seat. He pulled out a chair for himself and sat down a few yards from the group and apologised to Lisa, Sarah, Dawson and Stefan for them being here with the others.

"You're here purely as witnesses and that's all."

Mrs Holland sniffed indignantly and looked away from the lad. Obviously put out that she hadn't been included in the list or given an apology.

"The boy's been nothing but trouble since he got here," she spouted, "I should've seen this coming."

Edward asked for quiet.

"I'm going to ask you a question Mr Billingham, "he said, pointing the pistol directly at him and placing his finger on the trigger, "and if you lie I'll shoot you. Do you understand?"

Mr Billingham glared at him hatefully but eventually nodded.

"Did you kill my dad?"

The large bearded man glanced at DaSilva but said nothing as he defiantly glared back at Edward. The man had decided to call Edward's bluff. The lad smirked, aimed and pulled the trigger.

Wood splintered into the air as the lead burst through the back of the chair and Billingham jumped a foot in the air from the shock. The gunshot reverberated off every wall around them before quickly diminishing.

"Did you?"

Mr Billingham straightened his gold chains, along with his composure, before eventually nodding.

"Yes," he confessed, clearly surprised that the boy had pulled the trigger.

Both Lisa and Sarah gasped in unison and Dawson mumbled something to Stefan at the man's confession.

"And Charles Walker?"

"Yes."

Edward looked at Mr Carter and then at DaSilva before looking back at Billingham.

"Why?"

"For my part, revenge." sneered Billingham.

"And for him?" Edward asked, briefly flicking the barrel of the gun in DaSilva's direction, "What was his reason?"

DaSilva shook his head disappointedly, he knew Billingham was about to spill the beans.

"Keep schtum!" he sneered under his breath, grimacing at his bearded accomplice.

Billingham shrugged. "Not entirely sure," he replied, his eyes now on Armando, "But he was anxious to get rid of them both for some reason."

All eyes were now on Armando and he glanced at everyone around the table disdainfully. "He's lying!" he sneered, "The man's full of sheet."

Billingham's eyes widened with rage.

"It was your idea!" he snarled.

"All lies."

"The plan, the alibi, everything!"

"I'm innocent."

"Why, you................"

Billingham shot to his feet and clambered across the table towards DaSilva who struggled to get out of the way and toppled backwards in his chair. Within seconds the large man was on top of him, beating his face with a fist of gold rings.

"You're not pinning it all on me you lousy bastard," he cursed, struggling to stay on top of DaSilva, "You're just as guilty!"

DaSilva managed to grapple his way from beneath the bearded man and gain the upper hand for a moment, throwing several punches of his own. The two men wrestled around on the floor for a few minutes exchanging blows but stopped when Edward fired a second time, shattering a crystal decanter only a few feet from them.

"I would like nothing more than to watch you two kill each other," he shouted, getting their attention, "But I'm not finished with you yet."

DaSilva picked up his chair and flopped down exhausted onto it, his face was bleeding from several deep gouges and he kept his eyes fixed on Billingham. The large man made his way back around the table, his face slightly bruised around one eye.

Lisa and Sarah, who had moved away from the ruckus in fear of getting caught up in it, also returned to their seats.

"I hope you no longer think I'm insane?" Edward remarked, looking at them both as he waited for everyone to settle down again, "and realise why I'm doing this?"

"I'm worried about Marie," Sophia piped up, looking increasingly agitated by what was happening, "she'll be scared locked in her room all alone."

"Anxious to leave, are we?" Edward asked, sneeringly.

"The gun shots may have frightened her," came the reply.

Edward straightened his chair and sat himself down again.

"She's safer where she is," Mr Carter interjected, giving Sophia a knowing stare.

"Now that we know what really happened to my dad," he remarked, to his captive audience, "Let's find out what happened to my mom."

Mr Carter groaned loudly, "Oh, for god's sake, we already know what happened, " he huffed, impatiently, "Why are you still trying to twist this to suit you?"

"Twist this to suit me?" Edward snapped, "You're the one who's happy with their story because it suits you."

"Edward, everything that Mrs Simpson told me made complete sense. It has nothing to do with being happy about it or wanting it to suit me. It's about being the truth."

"A minute ago everyone thought Walker shooting my dad was the truth but now we know different, don't we? Now we know the real truth."

Frustrated, William gave a long and laboured sigh.

"Look, I know you want to find a connection between their deaths, Edward, and yes, now we know what really happened to Gareth but, what happened to Heather was a tragic accident and there's no one to blame."

Edward arched his brow with anger and clenched his teeth.

"The connection is Mr & Mrs Walker, and your wife and that bastard are to blame for everything." he snarled.

"Steady, lad," Dawson said, calmingly, "We don't want that thing going off again, do we?"

Edward slid his rucksack off his shoulders and grabbed the newspaper and diary from within it, throwing them onto the table. They landed in front of Sarah who was sat to his left and he asked her to read the news article about Mrs Walker.

Sarah did as she was instructed and when finished was then asked to read out the last entry in the diary. Everyone sat quietly and listened.

DaSilva was clearly getting agitated as he leant back in his chair staring at Edward, he knew the lad was looking for an excuse to kill him. Sophia and Mrs Simpson too were looking increasingly uncomfortable.

For the benefit of all those still in the dark

about the situation they now found themselves in, Edward explained everything as clearly as he could.

He told them how DaSilva had used Billingham to get rid of both his dad and Mr Walker, including the alibi story, and that it was all connected to his mother's passing seven years earlier. He then pointed out the fact that Mrs Carter had the jewellery she was wearing the day she went missing.

"She died in a fire with her aunt." Mr Carter interjected, glancing around at everyone defiantly, "We've already established that, Edward. Why can't you just accept it?"

"Because it's not true, that's why!" Snapped the lad, "and you know it."

He glowered at Sophia for a moment before demanding she told everyone about her drug addiction.

"That's what caused all this to happen!" he added, angrily, "That's why my parents are dead."

A wave of shocked gasps made their way around the table and Sophia welled up with tears.

"And he supplied her with them!" Continued Edward, pointing the pistol directly at DaSilva.

Armando was clearly ruffled and he looked at everyone in the hope that someone would question the boys actions, but to no avail. Sophia was sat with her hand to her mouth as if trying to hold in vomit but she remained silent.

The would be hit man, his chin dripping with

blood from his clash with Billingham, quickly weighed up his options. With Dawson, Stefan, Lisa, Sarah, Mrs Holland and Billingham sat on the opposite side of the table his choice was limited which made his decision easier to reach.

29

Mrs Simpson was the closest to him and he did what any self centred scumbag would, he grabbed the old woman by her dress and yanked her from the chair. She cried for help but the man was too strong for her and within a seconds he had his shield.

He lifted up his leg a little and grabbed a small knife, that had been concealed in a leather pouch strapped to his ankle, and forced Mrs Simpson away from the table with the blade to her throat.

Albert had jumped to his feet in an attempt to help her but stopped dead the moment he saw the knife. William too had been quick to his feet but realised almost instantly that there was nothing he could do.

The manoeuvre had happened so rapidly that Edward had been unable to respond in time to prevent it. He knew the man could not be trusted but his own growing confidence had made him complacent. He should have anticipated that the man would try something.

"Back off!" snarled DaSilva, as Mr Carter neared him.

Sophia yelled at him to let her go but her cousin pressed the blade harder into the old woman's neck. She whimpered as the edge sliced her skin.

"The boy's going to keel me no matter what!" he snapped, looking directly at Billingham, "and you'll be next."

Although shocked by what had just occurred, everyone but Lisa on the far side of the table had remained seated. They were sat wide eyed and agog but Lisa had made her way to the end of the table and was sobbing.

"And you think having that lying old bag as a shield is going to stop me?" Edward enquired stepping nearer, "Go ahead, slit her throat. I don't give a shit!"

"Edward!" shouted Lisa, pitifully, "That's my Nan!"

"I'm sorry but, she lied about my mom and she's as guilty as them!"

The old woman tried to disagree but DaSilva told her to keep her mouth shut as he continued to force her away from the group. She then said something that almost made Edward drop the pistol and which sent DaSilva into a rage.

"Your mother didn't die in that fire!" she croaked, struggling to speak from the weight of the knife, "she never left this hou................."

"Shut your face, woman!" snarled DaSilva, pressing the blade deeper into her neck and glaring at Sophia for help.

It was then that blood began to trickle down Mrs Simpson's chest, soaking into her white blouse, and Lisa screamed as her grandmother's body went limp in DaSilva's arms. As the old woman fell to the ground Lisa lunged forward to help her but ended up being DaSilva's second shield.

Again, the whole thing had happened so quickly that Edward, still trying to digest what the old woman had said, was not given enough time to intervene and watched helplessly as Lisa was manhandled into position. DaSilva grinned at Edward's pained expression.

"Geeve a sheet now?" he asked, sneeringly.

Albert dropped to his knees and tried to stem the flow of blood but the cut was so long and deep that the blood simply gushed through his fingers.

"Mildred!" he sobbed, trying in vain to help her, "Mildred!"

Sophia was also on her knees but she was quick to realise that help was futile, the blood had stopped pumping and the old woman was dead. Albert fell on top of her sobbing.

Sophia glowered at her cousin as she got to her feet. She looked furious and was trembling with anger. She knew that DaSilva had just ruined everything and that her life was now in tatters. William grabbed her arm and asked what Mrs Simpson had meant by her last words.

"Keep schtum, cuz," DaSilva told her, pressing the blade into Lisa's throat, "and you, put the gun on the table!"

"What did she mean?" William asked again, positioning himself between DaSilva and his wife and forcing her to look at him.

Lisa and Edward were locked in a gaze across the room. Tears were streaming down her face and her eyes were pleading for help. Edward was in turmoil because DaSilva now had someone he cared for and the tables had been turned. He was confused. Mrs Simpson's confession had threw him.

Sophia looked into her husbands eyes and began to sob uncontrollably before falling into his arms. It was obviously an act but William embraced her as if he was oblivious to it.

"Drop the gun!" DaSilva demanded again, tightening his grip on Lisa.

By now everyone had left their seats. Sarah had rushed to join Albert on the floor and was trying to comfort him. Dawson was making his way towards DaSilva followed closely by Billingham and Stefan had ventured nearer to Edward. Bautista had managed to stand but had not ventured from the table.

DaSilva warned them to back off and threatened to slit Lisa's throat if they took another step and Edward refused Stefan's request to relinquish the pistol.

"If I do, we're all dead." he explained, before telling him to stay put

Edward had a difficult decision to make. He knew that if he gave up the gun DaSilva would kill him, and probably everyone else along with him, and if he didn't then he would probably just manage to kill Lisa before being shot.

Mrs Simpson was lying dead on the floor because of his persistence to get to the truth and Lisa probably hated him and blamed him for it. Never the less, he wished her no harm but could not decide on what to do for the best.

"If you kill her you'll have no shield." he shouted, stating the obvious but wanting DaSilva to know he was thinking ahead, "and if you get the gun, you'll kill us all," he added, so that Lisa understood his reluctance to give it up.

His eyes were still fixed on hers and he watched her expression change ever so slightly as his words were digested.

"Only you!" DaSilva remarked, "I'll only kill you."

Sophia pushed herself away from William.

"There'll be no more killing!" she screamed, furiously, "Let her go, and you!," see added, pointing at the lad, "drop the gun!"

Both refused her demand. DaSilva in fear of being shot and Edward in fear of the psychopath getting his hands on the pistol.

"It's gone too far Armi," she snarled, stepping towards him, "Please, give me the knife."

Armando stared at his cousin and shook his head defiantly before glancing towards the door. It was clear that escape was his priority and he meant for Sophia to help him achieve it. She stepped aside to let him pass.

Slowly, he forced Lisa towards the door and everyone stood and watched helplessly. The girls neck was already bleeding and any sudden movement from anyone could result in death.

Edward could not let him leave and beat him to the door.

"You're not leaving until I know what happened to my mom!" he growled.

"Get out of my way or her blood weel be on your hands!"

"Then, I'll just get the truth from Sophia. Is that what you want?"

The two enemies glared at each other for a short while. They were now only a few yards apart and Edward was overwhelmed with the desire to shoot DaSilva. If he could get at clear shot of the mans shoulder his arm would drop like a stone, taking the knife with it but, the risk was too high.

"You can do whatever you like once I've gone!"

"You coward!"

"Eets all her fault anyway!"

Edward glanced over at Mrs Carter. Her face was like thunder but what caught his eye was the fact that the library door was now wide open and William was nowhere in sight.

Dawson, who was still in the dining room and peering into the library, turned to look at the lad. There was genuine concern on his face as he pretended to hold a rifle as if playing a game of charades.

Edward knew exactly what his friend was trying to tell him and the image of the glass cabinet with the rifles and shotguns sprang to mind. The tension had just been cranked up a notch and the question was, who would William shoot at first? It was now Edward who needed a shield.

He signalled to Dawson to bring Sophia to him but the man hesitated too long and William suddenly appeared behind him in the doorway.

30

"Drop the gun, Edward!" demanded William as he stormed back into the dining room, "and you, let Lisa go!"

With Edward's attention on the automatic rifle, DaSilva made his move. With one hefty shove he flung Lisa towards the lad and darted for the door. The girl stumbled into Edward's arms, preventing him from stopping DaSilva's escape, but he quickly pushed her aside in hot pursuit.

Mr Carter had not had time to react and watched angrily as they both fled from him, his attention turned to his wife.

By the time Edward had darted from the dining room DaSilva was already on the half landing. He turned to face the lad and skilfully threw his knife directly at him before continuing his escape. Instinctively, Edward managed to dodge the twirling blade and fired the pistol in retaliation.

The bullet ricocheted off the banister forcing DaSilva to crouch down as he ascended the stairs. Another shot was fired but Edward was now running after his quarry and the bullet was way off target.

He chased DaSilva upstairs.

The man had almost made it to his room by the time Edward had reached the first floor landing and he quickly fired a shot down the corridor indiscriminately.

The bullet clipped DaSilva's ear, causing him to stumble forward, but he managed to stay on his feet and disappeared into his room, slamming the door behind him and locking it.

Just then, a loud bang from down in the dining room, startled him and he looked back along the corridor in surprise. The gunshot was followed by hysterical screams and shouting before the dining room door opened.

Edward sprinted over to the atrium to peer down onto the hallway. Sophia had backed out of the room and was pleading with her husband not to shoot. William stepped into view with is smoking rifle trained directly at her.

Edward could hear sobbing and distressed murmurs coming from the dining room and knew that Mr Carter had shot someone, but who?

"Is what Albert said true?" he growled, red faced and tearful, "Tell me!"

Sophia was sobbing uncontrollably and refused to answer him. Holding her hands out in front of herself, as if hoping to block a bullet if he were to pull the trigger, she continued to back away.

"Tell me!" he snarled, lunging forward in a deliberate scare tactic.

Sophia squealed in fright and dropped to the floor submissively.

Edward had not heard what Albert had said

PAUL JACKSON

but, whatever it was, it had upset Mr Carter enough to threaten to kill his wife. He desperately tried to piece the puzzle together as he watched the drama unfold.

Bautista was now standing in the doorway and pleading with his brother in-law to lower the rifle but William was ignoring him. He stepped to one side so he could keep an eye on the fat man's movements.

"This is all that boy's fault," said Bautista, wobbling out into the hallway, "It's him you should be pointing that thing at."

The old hag's words were still swimming around Edward's brain and, all at once, pieces of the puzzle fell into place. The boy now knew that his mother had not died in the fire which meant that the body they found must have been Mrs Walker's. The few teeth that were found intact and the engagement ring at her side were put there to trick everyone.

Edward suddenly felt himself getting angry again and looked back at DaSilva's bedroom door. He stormed towards it blasting the lock as he neared and, with a hefty kick, the door swung open clattering against the return wall.

As Edward scanned the room from the threshold a knife whooshed passed his face and dug into the architrave, forcing the lad to duck and run for cover. He darted for the chair near the vent and crouched down behind it just as a second knife struck it.

Holding out his hand, he fired a couple of blind shots in DaSilva's direction before peering out from behind his shield. The man was cowering behind his bed and Edward stood up and trained the pistol at him

"Stand up!" Edward demanded, nearing the bed, "Stand up!"

Reluctantly, and while pressing one hand against his ear to stop the blood flow, DaSilva heaved himself up onto the edge of the bed as Edward walked around it to face him directly.

"What happened to my mom?" he asked, keeping a yard or two between them, "If she wasn't in the fire, then what happened to her?"

DaSilva, still grimacing with pain, looked at Edward but said nothing.

"You pulled her teeth out to make it look like it was her but the body was Mrs Walker's, wasn't it?"

Again, the scumbag remained tight lipped. His expression was one of self pity and not remorse. He wasn't sorry for what he'd done, just sorry that the truth was finally coming out. Edward looked into his dark shady eyes

The wretch was going to stay loyal to his cousin and had no intention of saying a word or answering any questions. He would rather die than betray his family. Perhaps his silence was born from his belief that Edward would not kill him and that he thought the lad hadn't got the balls.

Gritting his teeth in anger, Edward pulled the

trigger but to his utter shock nothing happened, the gun was empty.

31

Meanwhile ....

Sophia was still refusing to answer her husbands questions as she sat sobbing uncontrollably on the hallway floor. Several of the staff were now stood watching and Bautista was still trying in vain to get William to calm down.

"If she's not mine!" yelled Mr Carter, "I swear, I'll kill you both!"

"But, of course she's yours." Bautista offered, reassuringly, "Whatever's possessed you to think otherwise?"

William turned and glowered at his brother in-law.

"You heard what Albert said," he snarled, "It was her who had the termination, not Heather!"

For a moment, Bautista was shocked at William's accusation. He glanced down at his sister as he tried to recall what the old man had said.

"I only heard him say that a Mrs Walker had come to see Sophia," remarked the portly man, "As far as I'm aware, there was no mention of a termination."

Again, Bautista glanced down at his sister indignantly. His religion forbade abortions and knew his own sister would not have gone against that teaching, that would be sacrilege.

Tearfully, Sophia looked up at her brother. Her eyes were pleading for forgiveness and without words, Bautista could tell that she had suffered a great loss. Her sorrowful, pitiful, persona also led him to believe that, whatever she had done, it had not been by choice.

"He said it was her who needed that woman's services," William said, still glaring at Bautista, "and not Heather!"

Bautista frowned, "There's still no mention of a...................."

"Mrs Walker was an illegal abortionist." growled William, interrupting.

A gunshot from upstairs distracted everyone for a moment followed by the sound of a door clattering open. Edward had just gained access into DaSilva's room and all eyes were trained at the staircase for a moment as they listened. Even Sophia subdued her sobbing to hear.

It was following two more shots when Mr Carter finally asked Dawson to go and see if he could intervene. The grounds man nodded and quickly disappeared upstairs.

The interruption had given Bautista time to think. There had been no mention of when this abortion had taken place and the time frame had not been established.

"I cannot believe that Sophia would willingly terminate her pregnancy," he said, trying to keep William's attention on him once Dawson had gone, "and, even if she had, it was probably way before Marie was even born. Just because you think................"

"It happened seven months before she arrived!"

Again, Bautista frowned as he struggled to do the maths. William himself froze as the words fell from his lips, as if saying them out loud had clarified everything for him and the truth was realised. Slowly, he turned to look down at his wife with building rage. He now knew Marie could not be his and that Sophia had terminated his child. The question was, who's was she?

By the time Dawson had arrived at DaSilva's bedroom he found the two occupants engaged in a vicious brawl. They were entangled and rolling around on the floor. Edward was frantically clubbing DaSilva with the pistol on the head while being strangled and kneed in the ribs.

Dawson intervened with several heavy kicks into DaSilva's torso and eventually the man rolled away before jumping to his feet. His face was a mess, bruised and covered in blood with a ragged earlobe. Like a man possessed, he lunged for the sinewy grounds man.

Although tall and thin, Dawson was stronger than he looked and gave Armando as good as he got and the pair engaged in a vicious brawl of their own.

Edward picked himself up. He too was now bleeding, his lip had been split and there was a small gash across his left brow. He watched as DaSilva began to gain the upper hand over his friend and, dropping the gun, looked around for a better weapon.

Dawson was now reeling from a series of well aimed punches and was soon forced backwards onto the bed. DaSilva began to pummel him in a fit of rage, raining down punch after punch, but then stop suddenly and screamed out in agony. Dawson kicked him away and clambered to his feet.

Edward had stabbed his enemy in the back, just above his shoulder blade, and Armando frantically tried retrieving the knife as he stumbled away from them. As he neared the door he managed to yank it free and immediately flung it at the lad, turning to run as he did so.

The boy dodged the spinning blade and darted after him, followed closely by Dawson. Edward had a second knife in his hand, he'd not thrown one before and had no idea if he could but, as he gained on DaSilva he threw it.

The Portuguese hit man had almost reached the staircase when the dagger jabbed into his leg and then flew off somewhere across the landing. The impact was enough to slow him down and Edward gained on him rapidly.

The two collided which propelled DaSilva forward and sent Edward sprawling off to one side. The murdering low life collapsed at the head of the stairs but could not stop his momentum. He gambolled forward awkwardly down the stairs and crumpled onto the half landing, coming to rest on his backside, facing the hall and smashing one of the large urns in the process.

Sophia was a sobbing wreck at the foot of the stairs and William was standing on the half landing, his rifle pointing down at her, as DaSilva arrived.

"He's going to kill her, Armi!" she sobbed, as her cousin made his undignified entrance, "He's going to kill her!"

Mr Carter, dodging the shattering urn, diverted his aim at Armando.

"What happened?" he snarled, pushing the rifle into his face and looking back down at Sophia menacingly, "I demand to know the truth."

Out of breath, grimacing with pain and his face smeared in blood, he looked up at William.

"Eet all got out of hand," said DaSilva, dolefully, "We had no choice."

Sophia, shocked that her life was unravelling before her eyes, collapsed onto the first step and looked up at her cousin. Tears were streaming down her face and she was shaking her head and willing him to be quiet.

"There were complications and................" he trailed off as he lost himself in her eyes. He hated seeing her in pain.

"And!" William demanded, prodding him with the barrel again.

"Drugs!" Edward shouted down from the atrium, "I've already told you. She's was on drugs and still is!"

William glared up at the lad.

"This is all because of her addiction" Edward added, keeping partly obscured by the decorative wrought iron balustrade.

"Is that true?" Mr Carter asked, now looking down at Sophia.

She stared back at him for a short while before finally nodding and turning away ashamed. Slowly, she got to her feet. The room was silent and, realising her husband had not responded, turned back to face him in the hope he had not stormed off to Marie's room.

Relieved to see him still glaring down at her she wiped the tears from her cheeks and scraped the hair from her face.

"It had been difficult for me," she said, meekly, "With you away all the while with god knows who and me cooped up in here. I thought you'd spend more time with me once I was pregnant."

William arched his brow. "You saying this is my fault?" he growled.

"No, I'm just telling you where I was at the time. I was in a bad place."

"Oh, poor little Sophia. Being waited on hand and foot in this mansion and wanting for nothing!" sneered William, "It must have been terrible for you!"

"I thought you were playing the field!"

"You mean you were paranoid more like?"

She sniffed back more tears and wiped her nose

on her sleeve.

"Perhaps. But now you know why the drugs."

"And that's why you called for Mrs Walker?"

"Yes."

"Because you felt something was wrong?"

"Yes."

"The foetus was dead!" interrupted DaSilva, still looking into Sophia's eyes, "But, eenstead of just telling you, we covered eet up."

William lowered the rifle. His heart was breaking.

"She was terrified of what you'd do eef you ever found out," continued Armando.

"You should've just told me!" he said, his voice quivering.

"I was terrified of losing you!" Sophia snivelled, "The baby was going to fix everything between us but, finding out that I would never have the chance again, I had to do something!"

Realising he was in no danger from Mr Carter, Edward had been making his way down the stairs as the story unfolded. For him the penny had already dropped and the true reason why his mother hadn't died in the fire was clear.

"So you killed my mother and stole my sister!?" he hissed through gritted teeth.

32

A wave of gasps floated around the hallway and Sophia fell to her knees once more at the sound of Edward's words. They were like a hammer blow to her heart as the truth was revealed out loud.

"I'm a monster!" she yelled, "A monster!"

William, shell-shocked and angry, glared menacingly at Edward. The lad had been right all along, this whole nightmare had everything to do with Marie just as he had suspected. He lifted up the rifle and aimed it at him.

"This is all your fault!" he snarled, "and I curse the day I let you into my home!"

Taken by surprise, Edward stepped backwards, tripping onto the stairs and flopping onto his backside. He remained silent and daren't move, he knew William would not hesitate to shoot him if he did.

"You've been nothing but trouble ever since you arrived!" William continued, angrily.

"This isn't the lad's doing, sir." said Dawson, bravely stepping between them, "He didn't cause this he just bought it to light."

William kept the rifle steady. "Yes, exactly, and if he'd never come here none of this would be happening!"

"No, and you'd have gone on living with your head in the sand."

William glowered at him and, just for the briefest of moments, thought about pulling the trigger. "Better that than this!" he scowled.

"I feel your disappointment sir but, put yourself in Edward's shoes for just a moment. Both his parents have been murdered and his sister stolen."

Mr Carter continued to glare at him but said nothing.

"Who's the bigger victim here?" continued Dawson.

"Leave Edward be!" sobbed Sophia, looking up at him pitifully, "None of this is his fault!"

"No, eet's all yours!" admitted DaSilva, still grimacing with pain, "I should never have leestened to you!"

There was a short silent pause as all eyes were trained on Sophia until William asked, somewhat sympathetically towards her, what sex the baby had been.

"A boy," DaSilva informed him, answering for her.

"And where is he?"

"The basement."

"And Heather?"

The kissing cousins glanced guiltily at Edward before DaSilva replied. "The basement," he confessed.

Edward sprang to his feet and gripped DaSilva's throat with both hands.

"Did you kill her?" he snarled.

The memory of falling down into the basement was instantly rekindled as he remembered the feeling that someone had been nearby. A shiver ran up his spine as realised that he may have sensed her presence.

DaSilva, tight lipped and grimacing, gripped the boys wrists and slowly prised his hands from his throat.

"Did you kill her you bastard!?" Edward demanded, with venom in his voice, "Tell me!"

"No, he didn't," came a voice from across the hall. All eyes turned.

Albert was now standing in the dining room doorway covered in his wife's blood, there were streaks of it across his face where he had wiped his tears away. He looked ready to pass out.

"Mildred did!" he confessed, "but it was because of him!"

No one looked more shocked than Sophia who was now staring at her cousin questioningly. He glanced at her briefly before looking away. The heavy weight of guilt on his face was plain to see.

Just then, Stefan appeared in the doorway behind Albert and looked directly at Mr Carter before shaking his head.

"He's gone, sir!" he said, wiping blood down the front of his tank top.

Edward knew that Stefan was referring to Billingham, apart from Lisa he was now the only one missing from the group. There had been a gunshot earlier, just before he had stormed

DaSilva's room. Billingham must have tried something stupid and Mr Carter had shot him.

Knowing that the man who had killed his dad was now lying dead in the next room pleased him but another man who also deserved to die was still breathing.

Albert had made his way across the hall, his eyes only on Edward.

"I swear I had no idea!" he said, as he neared, "I only found out myself a few hours ago!"

Sophia, wanting answers and, still on her knees, grabbed the old man by his trouser legs to get his attention.

"What do you mean, it was because of him?" she snivelled, her eyes fixed firmly on Armando's guilt ridden face, "Heather died giving birth!"

DaSilva, his face still turned away from her, swallowed nervously and she knew that she was not going to like the answer to her question. Her cousin could not look more ashamed of himself.

"That's what he made Mildred tell you. He's the bigger monster!"

"What do you mean?" snarled Edward, confused.

"I mean he forced Mildred to say she'd died giving birth so that he could visit her whenever he wished."

Edward looked puzzled for a few moments until it dawned on him what Albert had meant. His bewildered expression quickly turned to rage and he lunged for DaSilva's throat again. There was a short violent struggle before Dawson grabbed Edward's shoulders, pulling him back up and away from the desperately flailing Armando.

"He's the killer, son, not you" he said, "Don't give him the easy way out."

"But, this filthy bastard raped her!?"

"And he'll spend the rest of his life in prison for it." offered his friend, "His death will haunt you forever, trust me!"

"He pulled her teeth out, Dawson," snarled the lad, tears dripping from his face, "he chained her in the basement, stole her baby and then raped her. He doesn't deserve the luxury of prison!"

He glared at Albert and growled "How long?"

The question went over the old man's head and he shrugged his shoulders.

"How long did it go on for? When did she die?" Edward bawled.

"I don't know, years probably, but as soon as Mildred found out what was happening, and knowing the poor woman had no other way out, she poisoned her."

"You knew she was still alive!" croaked DaSilva, looking at Sophia with blood-shot eyes, "Deep down, you knew!"

Edward and her husband both glared at her together, waiting for a reaction. She shook her head and swore she had no idea that Heather had survived the birth.

"I wouldn't have been able to stand by and do nothing!" she exclaimed, "If I knew what he was doing!"

"That's bullshit !" snapped Edward, "You kept her prisoner and stole her baby for fuck sake, and now you want me to think you cared about her 'well being' afterwards?"

"I honestly thought she'd died," sobbed Sophia, wiping her eyes, "I had no idea what was going on, but if I had I would've stopped him!"

"Were you going to let her go?" scowled the lad.

DaSilva huffed loudly as Sophia froze at the question, "Never!" he sneered, "How could we?"

William, completely devastated by what had transpired, sat down on the stairs with the rifle across his lap and his feet on the half landing. Dawson was right, Edward was the bigger victim here and understood the lad's desire to get to the truth, and his anger now that he had found it.

Edward was quick to seize the opportunity and sprang across the landing, swiping the firearm from the man's clutches. Within a heartbeat he had the rifle pressed hard against DaSilva's face.

Dawson grabbed the boys arm but Edward ordered him, and everyone else to stay put. Not wanting to cause the weapon to fire by accident the man let go.

"No one will blame you if you pull the trigger, Edward," William said, trying to stay calm, "But Dawson's right, it'll haunt you forever."

Grimacing with pure hatred, Edward glared down at DaSilva and wrapped his finger around the trigger.

"It will be a memory to treasure!" he sneered.

Just then, there was a knock at the door.

Everyone had been too distracted by what was occurring to have noticed the headlights sweep across the hallway and it had taken them all by surprise.

33

The hallway was instantly filled with panicked whispers as the group looked around at each other nervously, some waiting for instructions as to what to do with others slinking back into the dining room out of sight.

William sprang to his feet and Edward handed him back the rifle. Sophia ran to her brother while Albert disappeared back into the dining room, he was covered in blood and unable to answer the door.

In a matter of seconds the only two still standing in the hallway were Sarah and Mrs Holland, each nudging the other towards the door. Dawson and Edward had already dragged DaSilva up onto the first floor landing, leaving Sophia and Bautista to make their own way up behind them on the opposite flight. William remained on the half landing.

Sarah looked up at him and he nodded the instruction for her to see whom had arrived. Mrs Holland, clearly relieved, scurried back into the dining room with the others as Sarah, still wearing her apron, made her way to the door.

"May I help you?" she enquired, holding the door ajar just enough to show her face.

It was the Billingham brother's. They were enquiring about their father.

"He said to come back for him within the hour," explained the taller of the two, "and it's been longer than that," added the other, half-wittedly.

As they spoke, Sarah eyed a few shadowy figures behind them, lingering in the darkness by the statue of cupid. She was sure that they were carrying weapons. The boys had come armed and ready for trouble.

"The meeting hasn't finished yet," explained Sarah, ad-libbing, "I can pass a message on and get him to call you later if you wish?"

The boys looked at each other for a moment, they were suspicious and unwilling to leave.

"You mean go home, wait for the phone call and then come back?" sneered the young man.

Sarah nodded and smiled.

"That would mean a forty minute round trip. No, we'd rather come in and wait, if it's all the same to you?" he insisted, sliding one foot across the threshold, "They can't be much longer."

By now, William had made his way over to the door and was standing behind it listening. He had just killed their father and knew that things were about to get complicated.

He could hear several voices outside in the foreground and knew the lads had come prepared. Sarah would not be able to hold them back much longer.

Taking a deep breath, he swung open the door and forced the barrel of the rifle under the chin of the nearest brother. The other one stepped back a few paces as he pulled a pistol from the belt of his jeans.

With the barrel pressed against his jaw, The lad froze and glowered hatefully at William.

"I'm sorry Tristan," said Mr Carter, his eye on the shorter sibling who had called for back-up, "but there's been an incident and I need you to stay calm so that I can explain."

With the rifle in one hand, William held out the other and asked Tristan for his gun. The lad obliged as his brother asked what was going on. He was flustered and confused.

"Should I shoot, Tris?" he gasped, "shall I kill him?"

By now there were several figures standing nearby with William in their sights but, with Tristan as a shield, he knew they would be reluctant to fire.

"Tell them to back off, son!" ordered William, handing the lads gun to Sarah, "I promise I won't hurt you and I can explain everything."

Grimacing, Tristan glowered at Mr Carter for a short while before holding up his right hand as a sign to the others to hold back. He knew that Mr Carter was going to ask him in and he needed to know what had happened.

His younger brother protested but Tristan confirmed his order.

"Stay back Jez," he mumbled against the barrel of the rifle, "If I'm not out in ten minutes come in, guns blazing."

"You've gorrit," replied Jeremy, as his older brother disappeared inside, "I'll get the place surrounded."

Mr Carter took several steps backwards to allow Tristan to enter and Sarah closed the door behind him. The lad could hear voices coming from a room to his left and had already eyed several shadows moving about on the landing above.

"My brother's not good at keeping time so you'd better be quick." he sneered, "What's happened?"

William stepped aside and signalled with the rifle for Tristan to make his way into the dining room.

"I'm sorry lad," said Mr Carter, as the young man stood at the threshold, "but, it was an accident."

Albert and Stefan were the first ones he saw, both covered in blood with doleful expressions, he then saw an old woman lying dead with a young maid sobbing at her side.

He scanned the room for his father before spotting a pair of legs on the floor, jutting out at the far end of the table. He recognised the shoes immediately and gasped as he turned to face Mr Carter.

"He's dead?"

William nodded but said nothing.

Tristan stood glaring down at the legs for a moment, contemplating on whether to approach them or not. The pool of blood surrounding the old woman eventually convinced him to stay put.

"What happened?" he asked, glancing at Mrs Simpson's body, "Did he kill that woman?"

"No, DaSilva did," Mrs Holland informed him. She was sat at the table behind Stefan and Albert and had leant back in her chair to see around them.

"Slit her throat in cold blood he did," she added.

"And my dad?" he snivelled.

The head cook sheepishly glanced at Mr Carter before shaking her head and ducking back behind Albert and Stefan. The lad turned to face William.

"I was trying to calm things down but he grabbed the rifle." confessed Mr Carter, "He yanked it towards himself with my finger still on the trigger. There was nothing I could do, it was an accident."

"So, this is all DaSilva's fault?"

William looked around at everyone in the room before answering. He wanted to say yes but knew it was a lie. It had been Edward who had forced the issue but the true explanation was complicated. He looked back at Tristan and nodded.

"Where is he?"

"He's with Edward Kane!" Mrs Holland piped up, still hidden by Albert and Stefan, "Up stairs and taken hostage!"

Everyone shushed her and turned to face the bitter head cook. She sniffed and looked away. "This is all the boy's fault." she added.

Tristan's eyes widened. "Gareth Kane's son?" he questioned, looking over at the old woman, now without her human shield. She nodded, but didn't dare look back at him in case she met with the disgruntled glares of the others.

Tristan stood and pondered for a moment before being distracted by the sound of breaking glass. No one said a word as they listened to loud excited voices getting nearer and nearer. His impatient brother had found a way in.

Before long, someone appeared in the hallway from the snooker room corridor followed by someone else appearing from the library. Each was armed and instantly set their sights on Mr Carter. The tables had turned.

A tearful Tristan looked at William as he held out his hand and, reluctantly, Mr Carter gave the young man his rifle. Jeremy, now standing in the doorway of the library, was looking down at his father's corpse, frozen to the spot. Tristan made his way towards him.

One by one, the room slowly filled with the Billingham brother's gang, all glaring down in shock at the body of their boss. One had a gun pressed against Mr Carter's back and had forced him deeper into the room and another had forced Lisa to her feet and was leering at her.

The brothers consoled themselves with a hug, whispering to each other and glancing back at Mr Carter now and then as they decided on their next move. Tristan had been relieved to see that someone had covered his father's face with a jacket and was able to look down at him as the brothers talked.

"Edward Kane!" Jeremy suddenly blasted, attracting everyone's attention, "Where the fuck is he, I'll kill him!"

34

The unwelcome guests filed out of the dining room and into the hall as they followed the brother's. Jeremy had Lisa by the hair and immediately shouted up to Edward.

"Come down Kane or the maid gets it." he snarled.

Edward and Dawson were still crouched behind the atrium balustrade struggling to restrain DaSilva as they listened. Dawson had the man in a head lock with his hand over his mouth.

However, and before Edward could decide what to do, two of the Billingham gang had made their way onto the half landing and already had them in their sights. Dawson knew that it would be futile to try anything stupid and let go of DaSilva.

The man clambered to his feet, pushing the grounds man aside before holding onto the balustrade. Seeing his own blood had made him sick and unsteady. By now the two gang members were on the landing and ordered the trio down to the hall.

With a pistol in his back, Edward was forced to lead. Everyone watched as he descended the stairs and made his way towards the brothers. Lisa, terrified and with her head held to one side by her hair, stood in shocked silence.

"So, you're Kane's son?" sneered Jeremy,

looking the lad up and down disdainfully as he approached, "I've been looking forward to meeting you, ever since DaSilva told me about you that is."

Edward had not taken his eyes off Lisa. Even with mascara smudged eyes, red snotty cheeks and bedraggled hair, she still managed to look beautiful to him.

"You can let her go now!"

Jeremy, sensing the boys feeling towards the girl, laughed and yanked her head even lower. "No chance!" he snarled, "I'm going to make everyone pay for what you've done to my dad."

He stepped forward to be face to face with Edward. Jeremy was only an inch or two taller than him but was heavier built. He glowered into the lads eyes.

"But first, I'll start with that revenge I was promised."

Before long, the brothers had formed a makeshift ring using the members of the household and their gang, even forcing Sophia and Bautista down to participate. DaSilva sat and watched on the stairs.

Jeremy slid off his jumper and t-shirt and told Edward to do the same. The lad obliged and made his way to the centre of the hall. He looked over at Tristan.

"I am allowed to win?" he asked, sarcastically.

Tristan, surprised at first at the lads nerve, laughed before looking at his brother. Jeremy had ignored the comment and was warming up by going through a set of boxing manoeuvres.

Edward stood and watched. The display was meant to unsettle him but the rules of the fight had not been agreed. The stocky lad had clearly trained as a boxer but how was he at martial arts? Gareth had trained his son well.

Once Jeremy had finished his routine a member of the gang made a bell sound and the fight was on. After a couple of failed lunges by Billingham, the pair circled around the room for a moment or two, weighing each other up.

Edward allowed the lad to lunge forward again with a wild haymaker, dodged to the side and landed a jab to his ribs. Jeremy winced but swung his arm out wildly catching Edward in the back of the head.

The lad sprawled forward and managed to stay on his feet but Jeremy followed through with another blow. Edward went down, sliding towards DaSilva and prompting cheers from members of the gang.

The lad looked up at the Portuguese scumbag who, despite the loss of blood, was smirking down at him. Edward knew that, even if he won the fight, the brother's would kill him to avenge their father. He had nothing to lose and DaSilva's smirk had helped fuel his building rage.

This man had killed his parents as if they were nothing, he hated everything about him, his black greasy hair, his loathsome, greasy face, his thin brown lips.

He jumped to his feet and thumped Armando as hard as he could across his jaw. The man flopped backwards before slumping, unconscious, onto his side. Edward then turned to face Jeremy, his rage clear to see.

He darted towards the stocky lad, jumped into the air, spun around and kicked Jeremy in the side of his head. The lad stumbled backwards and crashed onto his backside, completely bewildered. The crowd fell silent.

Edward gave his enemy no time to recover and quickly stamped his foot into his chest, followed by one to his face. Like someone possessed, he straddled his enemy and proceeded to pummel him, jabbing his thumbs into his eyes and clawing at his face.

Tristan managed to grab the crazed lad and flung him off his helpless brother. Edward slid across the floor towards DaSilva and saw his chance to flee, pushing through the crowd and mounting the stairs.

He had taken everyone by surprise and a few seconds had passed before someone had the mind to follow him. Eventually, a large, heavily tattooed gang member ran after him followed closely by Tristan.

As they reached the first floor landing, Edward was already disappearing down the corridor to DaSilva's room and the gang member took a shot at him. The bullet whizzed through his hair but the lad continued to run.

By the time the pair had reached the door Edward had already slid a chair beneath the handle blocking it shut. Tristan and his accomplice frantically threw themselves against and eventually managed to dislodge the blockade. Billingham, entered the room, quickly scanning around for his quarry. The place was a mess from the earlier battle but it was the curtains, swaying in the breeze, that caught his eye.

He ran to the French doors and leant against the Juliet balcony as he looked out across the flat roof of the extension before looking across at the barn opposite. He recalled that DaSilva had mentioned that the lad was living in a barn.

Spotting the wall that linked the buildings he ordered his accomplice to make his way across it.

"Oh, and Dan, I want him alive!" snarled Tristan, breathlessly.

Edward, trying hard to suppress his own heavy breathing, watched them from within the secret passage. He'd managed to block the door, retrieve the pistol, open the French doors and scramble through the vent just in time. The door clattering open had masked his clumsy fumbling with the grille.

Tristan searched the room a little longer and Edward waited for him to leave before daring to move himself. He needed to get to his rucksack that was down in the dining room, it had the bullets for the gun in it.

35

Everyone had been ordered into the snooker room by the time Tristan had returned from upstairs and Jeremy, bruised and bloody faced, was waiting for him as he entered.

Apart from Mr Carter, all the members of the household had taken seats while some of Billingham's men had set the snooker table up for a game. William had also been waiting anxiously for Tristan's return.

"I think we should call the police before this goes any further " he suggested, approaching the brothers before they'd had time to speak, "I'll explain everything to them and leave out that you were even here."

Jeremy shook his head in protest and pushed his older brother aside.

"No, I want that little bastard to pay!" he snarled, "Look what he's done!"

He turned to face his brother. "Where is he?" he demanded.

Shrugging his shoulders, Tristan, explained how the lad had given them the slip and that he'd sent Big Dan to the barn to look for him.

"I think you should all leave before you do something you regret," William interjected, "Something that cannot be undone!"

Jeremy glowered back at William.

"You've killed my dad!" he snarled, prodding the man in his chest "Kane brain damaged my uncle and his son has done this to me! No way am I leaving until everyone gets what's coming to them!.

"What happened to your dad was an accident," explained Mr Carter, restraining his anger at being poked, "and your uncle knew the risks when he took the fight, he wasn't forced to, and it was no one's fault."

"Kane was a professional and shouldn't have been in the competition!"

William shook his head. "Gareth's ability at fighting was common knowledge by everyone and it was always their goal to beat him, but he was no professional."

Jeremy's building rage was obvious as he became more and more agitated, and was almost foaming at the mouth.

"He's humiliated me!" he growled, looking back at his brother for support, "Done this to my face and humiliated me, I want him dead!"

Tristan, slightly alarmed by the fury of Jeremy's rage, tried to calm him. He was angry himself but unsure about what to do next. He also wanted Edward dead, revenge for their uncle, but the plan had been to do it during the competition and out of sight.

"Make it look like an accident!" DaSilva had told them.

He knew, that if his brother had the chance, he

would kill Edward in front of everyone and there would be no going back from that. Mr Carter was right.

He pulled Jeremy to one side and, whispering, tried to explain the situation to him but the lad was having none of it.

"You mean leave?" he snarled, "Go home and pretend this never happened?"

Tristan nodded. "For now, yes."

"But, what about dad? He's lying dead in the next room!"

"Yes, I know, and Mr Carter will answer for it."

Fuming with rage, Jeremy pushed his brother aside again and set his sights on Mr Carter. The man had pulled the trigger and had not even been punished for it yet. The lad knew that if William managed to convince the police it was an accident he never would be.

He lunged for him wildly but Mr Carter was no fool. He had read the situation well, anticipating Jeremy's next move. As the lad came towards him he braced himself before thumping him full in the stomach. Winded, the lad crumpled to the ground.

In response, a member of the gang ran towards Mr Carter with his revolver pointed directly at him. Tristan was quick to intervene and managed to deflect the weapon just as the trigger was pulled. The bullet disappeared through the ceiling and Lisa screamed at the deafening gunshot.

"Stop!" Tristan yelled, eyeing another gang member running towards them, gun poised.

"Stop!"

Luckily, the man obeyed but Jeremy, still winded had managed to stand upright and frantically yanked the gun from his fingers, aimed and pulled the trigger. However, and to his utter shock, Tristan had tried to stop him.

By now, Edward, had made his way down beneath the half landing of the staircase and was peering through the access door near the dining room. He had heard the gunshots and screams and was eager to reach his rucksack.

Gingerly, he emerged near the snooker room corridor and quickly scanned around for anyone before darting across the hallway. He was grateful that the Brothers hadn't had the brains to keep someone on guard.

As he pulled his bag from the back of the chair he gawped at Mrs Simpson's, blood pooled, corpse. He had no pity at all for the old woman only the depressing thought that Lisa would never forgive him for getting her killed. The hag deserved what she got, there was no doubt in his mind about that, but he was sorry that Lisa had watched her die so gruesomely.

He loaded the pistol before throwing the bag over his shoulder and making his way into the library. He had remembered the door that led to the rear extension and had dared himself to peer through it. He had to know what was happening, to see if Lisa, Sarah and Dawson were unharmed.

He paused briefly at the open gun cabinet where two rifles and a pump action shotgun were on display. He was curious to see if there were more bullets that would fit his pistol but, finding the top drawer empty and lower ones locked, soon turned his attention back to the door adjacent to the cabinet.

Opening it as softly as possible, Edward peered through the gap, unseen, at the occupants within. Almost everyone in the room was standing with their backs to him and looking down at something at their feet.

The room was deathly quiet for a minute as different members of the Billingham gang knelt down behind the crowd before reappearing again shaking their heads and backing off.

"They're dead," said one of them eventually as he looked around at everyone, "They're both dead."

As if her legs could no longer carry her, Sophia, collapsed onto a nearby sofa and both Sarah and Lisa rushed to comfort her. Now, through the gaps created in the crowd, Jeremy could be seen kneeling at two bodies on the floor. He was holding the hand of one of them and sobbing.

Edward closed the door as carefully as possible once he had recognised the second corpse. He instinctively knew that, with both Mr Carter and Tristan now dead, Jeremy's rage towards him was about to escalate.

The stocky lad had gone way too far and now had nothing to lose. There was no one left who'd dare try to calm him and his loyal thugs would probably relish the hunt.

Edward was not only concerned for his own safety. He knew that every member of the household was now in grave danger because Jeremy could not afford to leave a single witness alive.

He had already forced Edward to give himself up when threatening to kill Lisa and he knew he would try the same tactic again. Billingham seemed unable to control himself and with no one here to quell his rage the situation could easily become a bloodbath.

Calling the police was the obvious decision and Edward made straight for the telephone on Mr Carter's desk but was horrified to find that the line was dead. Jeremy must have cut it before breaking into the house. He had initiative after all and was not as dumb as he looked.

It was then Edward realised that the library wasn't exactly the safest place to be and that he could be discovered at any moment. Cautiously, he made his way back across the dining room but was forced to dart behind the open door.

Edward had heard footsteps and voices coming from the snooker room and, with bated breath, he froze to the spot and peered out through the gap between the hinges.

By chance, Big Dan was now making his way across the hall as the two men appeared at the dining room doorway and he informed Jeremy that Edward could not be found.

"I turned the place upside down," he added.

"Do you think he's scarpered?" asked the other gang member, a thin, bearded yob with facial tattoos, "Gone for the cops or something?"

Jeremy took a deep breath as he pondered the question and sniffed back tears.

"No." he remarked, shaking his head, "He likes that maid too much to leave, he's still here alright."

Big Dan was already looking towards the snooker room, his curiosity gripped by the distant commotion but, before he had time to move, Jeremy grabbed his arm.

The grieving brother explained what had happened and that the situation was now dire but the big lad yanked his arm free and ran to his friend.

Jeremy, clearly narked, watched him disappear.

"Be ready for anything, Scut," he told his, self inked, accomplice sternly, "we might have a problem."

"Don't worry Jez, I've got your back."

36

Edward was relieved when Jeremy decided to head back to the snooker room, taking Scut with him. He took a deep breath and relaxed a little.

It was now clear to him that the Billingham gang were actually two separate factions, each loyal to one brother, and with Tristan dead, Jeremy was unsure what his brother's gang would do.

They could either join him, kill him or leave and Edward knew that their decision would not take long. He could already hear them arguing.

Cautiously, he made his way over to the staircase and quickly bolted up to the first floor landing. Until now, Marie had been quite safe locked in her room but, Edward knew that with a full scale search for him she would soon be in danger.

It sickened him to think that he may have lost his chance of saving Lisa or the others but he was determined to keep Marie out of harm's way.

He clambered through the loose vent that had revealed the twitten to him shortly after his arrival to the manor. Unfortunately, it now seemed even less secure than before but he managed to balance it in place.

As he made is way along the passage towards Marie's room he became aware that someone was mounting the stairs. He paused and listened for a moment as he tried to work out which way they were going. A small creak of a step told him that, whoever it was, had turned right at the half landing and was headed in the direction of DaSilva's room.

Relieved, he hurried along in the darkness, instinctively leaping across the gap in the boards before being forced to pause once more. There were now voices very close by and to his horror were heading towards Marie.

It was obvious that a search party had been sent to hunt for Edward and members of both gangs were probably scouring the entire house looking for him. All armed and looking for blood.

Reaching the vent to the room that held the little girl captive he hesitated briefly as he spied inside. Marie was sitting up on the edge of a single bed and gawping at the door. She too had heard someone approaching.

Edward prised the clips and forced the metal vent free, placing it on the floor before Marie saw him. Surprised, she jumped to her feet holding her teddy-bear tightly to her chest as she backed towards the door.

Grateful that she had not screamed, Edward reminded her of who he was and asked her to trust him.

"There's someone coming for you," he explained, "You'll be safer with me."

"I want my mom," she sobbed, shaking her head defiantly, "I want my mom!"

"Please, they're nearly here. Hurry!"

The little girl stood firm, shaking her head stubbornly.

"I'll protect you, Marie. Please!"

He held out his hands welcomingly but still the frightened child refused to budge. The voices neared. Doors were heard creaking open and before long they were almost outside.

They could be heard questioning Mrs Bautista in the adjacent room for short while but the moment her door handle rattled, Marie bolted towards Edward, who wasted no time in pulling her through the hole, unceremoniously. He dropped her to the boards before fumbling with the vent cover.

The bedroom door burst open and slammed back against the wall where only a few seconds before Marie had stood. Two gang members entered the room and began to rummage. One was a ginger haired guy armed with a pistol and the other a bald mixed race guy wearing spectacles.

They were now discussing the events that had taken place downstairs and Edward hovered at the vent to catch what they said. It was evident that neither was happy with what Jeremy had done and both felt they had been forced into a situation that was going to be difficult to get out of.

"I'd do a runner if I could," said the ginger guy, crouching down to look under the bed, " but he'd hunt me down if I did."

"There's not a lot we can do about it, Red" said

the other guy, scanning the room, "I'll just be glad when it's all over."

Red, checked inside the wardrobe before turning to his mate, "This'll never be over. How do you think this is going to end?"

His friend shrugged. "No idea."

"Do you think Jez is going to leave witnesses?"

Again, his answer was a bewildered shrug.

"They all saw him kill his own brother and that Mr Carter guy. Those people down there are all dead and they know it."

Edward looked down at Marie the moment her father was mentioned. His eyes had grown accustomed to the dark and could see her looking back at him with welling tears.

Edward tried to muffle her mouth, worried she would cry out, but she pulled away. Somehow, she managed to stifle herself but their panicked movements had not gone unnoticed.

The thugs were both looking down at the vent by the time Edward peered back through it. Red had his pistol trained directly at him.

"Come out," he ordered, approaching cautiously, "I won't hurt you."

His colleague noted that pointing the gun at a little girl wasn't exactly comforting.

"But it might not be the girl, Carl." replied Red, squinting down at the grille. "I mean, how would she even know how to remove the cover never mind replace it again?"

Carl frowned as he tried to work out what Red

PAUL JACKSON

had meant.

"You mean, it's Edward?"

By the absence of any screws, Red had already deduced that the grille would probably prise off if pulled and stretched out his hand towards it.

He told Carl to ready himself as his finger tips curled around the edge of the vent.

"What if we hit her?" Carl enquired, training his pistol at the grille, "I'm not shooting a little girl, Red!"

"Relax, they've probably bolted by now,"

Red could now feel the grille moving forward as he applied more pressure and knew it's removal was imminent.

"I think it's best if we just tell Jezza where they are." added Carl, clearly reluctant to participate.

"And say what, exactly!" scoffed Red, "That we were too scared to remove a vent so we let them go!"

Carl nodded.

Cursing under his breath, Red quickly glared at his colleague disdainfully before looking back down at the grille.

"Get fucking ready!"

And with that, Red prised off the vent forcing Carl to react.

Within the blink of an eye he found himself training his gun at the hole and gazing into the darkness but Red, fully expecting a confrontation, thrust his pistol forward and blindly squeezed the trigger.

The two men anxiously glared into the hole, both surprised that Red had fired without warning, and waited for a response. They watched the smoke clear before moving closer.

Edward, who had managed to escort Marie to a safe distance, had just returned when the shot rang out and had dropped to his knees in shock, glaring up at the hole above.

For the sake of his sister he knew he had to regain his composure quickly and swallowed back a nervous lump in his throat as he picked himself up. With his pistol poised he neared the hole.

Knowing that Jeremy would not leave anyone alive to bear witness to what had happened, Edward was fully prepared to kill whoever got in his way. His priority now was to protect Marie at all costs.

Luckily for him, Marie had not screamed and he had not made enough noise when cowering from the bang to alert the two thugs of his presence and he watched as the barrel of Red's gun appeared through the aperture.

With his heart racing he positioned himself directly below it and inhaled a breath of courage before enacting his hastily formed plan.

Waiting for the pistol to fully appear, Edward suddenly made a grab for it as he sprang to a standing position. He managed to force it sideways and back against the wall as he aimed his own gun and fired blindly into the room.

He felt Red's grip on the pistol loosen

immediately as he fired again indiscriminately and the man dropped out of sight. Edward's focus was now suddenly on Carl who had already fired back at him, narrowly missing his face.

Again, Edward unloaded another round of bullets, too panicked to aim properly, and somehow managed to hit his target. He heard Carl's pistol hit the floor and then watched the wild eyed man reeling backwards from the room, trying desperately to stop the blood gushing from his neck.

Edward reached in for the vent cover and replaced it he then retrieved Red's pistol from the twitten floor and, tucking it into the waistband of his trousers, made his way back to Marie.

37

Reacting to the gunfire, Jeremy ran out into the hallway glaring up at the atrium as he approached the foot of the stairs, followed closely by several gang members.

He had only sent out the search party a few minutes earlier and was surprised at how quickly something had happened.

"Did you get him?" he bawled excitedly, "is he alive?"

Big Dan was already at the half landing before someone had shouted back a reply.

"They're dead." came the cry, "He's killed Carl and Red."

Jeremy ordered Scut back to the snooker room to watch the captives before mounting the stairs to take a look for himself.

Carl had bled to death outside the bedroom door and Red was lying with his face against the window seat with two bullets in his face. Jeremy scanned the room before turning to face the person who had shouted back the reply.

"Did you see where he went?"

The youth, a skinhead with a goatee, shrugged his shoulders in response.

"See who?" he questioned.

"Edward, you fuckwit! Did you see him?"

The skinhead shook his head. "I was at the

other end." he replied, pointing towards DaSilva's room on the opposite side of the stairs.

Big Dan frowned. "You never saw him at all?"

Again, the skinhead shook his head.

"Where were you when you heard the shots?"

"Outside that end room," came his reply, "I saw Carl drop and I ran straight here."

Both Jeremy and Big Dan looked at each other before scanning the scene again but before they could draw their own conclusion a soft thud somewhere near the stairs was heard. The loose grille had finally given way.

Within seconds, Edward's secret twitten was discovered and Jeremy sent the skinhead inside to hunt him down with orders to kill on sight as Big Dan quickly checked the remaining rooms.

Dan shook his head as they met again in the corridor, "No sign of him," he said, now looking down at Carl's bloody corpse. "What shall we do with the bodies? They're mounting up."

"Don't worry about them," replied young Billingham as he made his way back to the stairs, "The fire will take care of it."

He made his way down to the hallway, shouting instructions to a few straggling gang members loitering around aimlessly.

"Don't just stand there gawping, find Edward Kane!" he bawled, heading for the snooker room, "and someone go outside and check the grounds."

The bodies of Tristan and Mr Carter had been covered with a throw-over from one of the sofas but were still lying where they fell. Sophia was being comforted by Sarah as she stared numbly down at her husband.

The other members of staff had all taken seats and were being guarded by Scut and another menacing thug who could not take his eyes off Lisa. She was sat motionless next to her grandfather, her hand in his and with her eyes fixed on her lap. She dare not move in fear of being singled out again.

Stefan, Mrs Holland and Dawson were all sat in the adjacent sofa while Bautista and DaSilva had bagged armchairs each and were sat a little further into the room. DaSilva, although still in some pain, seemed to be recovering from his wounds. Less melancholy and more alert.

The room was cold. A curtain wafted gently from the breeze through the shattered patio doors and everyone was dithering slightly.

All eyes turned to Jeremy as he entered the room and Sophia, pushing Sarah aside, sprang to her feet.

"Marie?" she questioned, anxiously.

Young Billingham scowled, "Kane has her."

"My god, he'll get her killed. I know it."

"No he won't., Mrs Carter." Dawson piped up, trying to calm the woman before she had time to escalate, "He'll keep her safe."

Sophia glowered down at the grounds man. "What, at gun point?"

"He's a smart kid."

"Smart kid! He's just dragged her into a war for Christ's sake!"

"Saving her from the inevitable more like."

Sophia, still glowering down at Dawson, stifled a reply as Sarah took her by the hand and applied a little pressure to encourage her to sit.

Bautista, his hand aloft, asked after his wife once his sister had finally taken her seat and Young Billingham, clearly narked, snapped back a reply.

"She's alive," he snarled, "for now!"

Looking at Sarah, Sophia asked her what Dawson had meant by his last remark but was shouted down by Jeremy. He had heard their conversation and knew exactly what the grounds man was getting at.

"What do you think he fucking meant?"

Sophia squeezed Sarah's hand tightly at the sudden outburst.

"Surely you know how this ends?"

Jeremy, not waiting for a reply, ordered Scut to take Lisa into the hall. The poor girl clung to her grandfather for dear life as the yob approached but he yanked her by the hair and pulled her towards him. She screamed as the other thug, still glaring at Lisa, helped to part them.

"You're wasting your time." DaSilva informed him, just as Dawson sprang to his feet to intervene. "The leetle girl ees his sister and no one een this room ees worth a damn to him."

Jeremy glowered at Armando for a moment before looking down at Mrs Carter. It took another moment or two before the penny finally dropped.

"Edward's your son?"

Tearful, Sophia shook her head.

"But Marie?"

Again, Mrs Carter shook her head before burying her face in her hands and sobbing. Dawson, with Scut's gun trained on him, sat back down.

"Eets a long story," DaSilva added, "but believe me, threats to kill any of them will no longer work."

"Since when were you bothered about these people?"

"My beef was with Edward, not them."

The events of the evening had happened so quickly and Jeremy had not had time to make sense of it all. His father's body was in the next room and his brother was lying dead at his feet. The details were blurred but he knew that it was DaSilva who had called his father.

"I should kill you first for getting my dad killed," he growled, "It's your fault he's dead."

"I was forced to call him here at gun point."

While young Billingham's attention was elsewhere, Sarah slid her hand into the front pocket of her apron. She still had Tristan's pistol hidden there and gripped it nervously. She had never fired a gun before but now, realising her fate if she did nothing, tried to build up the courage to act.

By now, Lisa had been forced towards the

door and Scut was awaiting further instructions as he stood observing the goings on. His lecherous friend was at his side, his hand around the young maids arm.

Jeremy trained his pistol at Armando for a moment.

"You said, WAS," he commented, "Your beef WAS with Edward. You've had a change of heart then?"

"A change een circumstance, perhaps. Eet's complicated."

"You no longer want him dead?"

DaSilva shrugged. "I deed."

"And now?"

"And now eet doesn't matter so much."

"It matters to me!"

Lowering the gun, Jeremy glanced around at his captives before making his way towards Lisa. Sarah watched as he turned his back to them, she knew she had hesitated too long already but could not bring herself to shoot the young man.

What if she missed, or the gun jammed? He would end up killing everyone there and then in a fit of rage and she would be to blame but, she had to help Lisa. The young maid was being led to her death.

Trying to control her breathing and with her heart pounding in her chest, Sarah suddenly decided to go for it and pulled the pistol from her apron.

However, Dawson had been watching her get

more and more agitated and had spotted the handle of the pistol well before she had acted. To her relief, he quickly grabbed it from her and sprang to his feet.

Within the blink of an eye both Jeremy and Scut were dead and their lecherous friend was cowering against the wall, his pistol poised to shoot.

Lisa, screaming hysterically, ran back to her grandfather while everyone else just sat and stared as Dawson dispatched the third young man before rushing to close and bolt the door to the hallway.

Other members of the Billingham gang would soon be here and he knew a shoot out was inevitable. Thanks to Sarah, their situation had changed but time was of the essence.

Grabbing the fallen pistols, Dawson made his way to the door that led to the library and wasted no time in bolting it shut. He then led everyone outside to the garden through the broken patio doors.

38

Edward knew that getting outside was his best bet for survival and had made straight for the wooden grille. He had already removed one of the slats before he heard someone approaching them in the twitten.

With Marie riding piggyback, he had clumsily bumped against the loose vent cover, knocking it free, and he knew it was because of that his hidden twitten had been discovered and someone was now hunting them within it.

As he removed the second slat a clatter rang out ahead of them. Whoever was approaching had not seen the hole in the floor around the metal ladder and, like Edward, had clambered frantically to prevent a fall.

It gave him enough time to lower Marie through the gap and onto the flat roof before sliding through himself. Frantically, he fumbled with the slats as he tried to insert them back into place before being discovered.

He had just managed to pull the second slat into position when he saw someone pass by. He ducked away and listened as they continued down the twitten unaware of his presence.

With a sigh of relief, Edward scanned the flat roof for movement. It was good to be out of the building and no longer trapped like a rat with nowhere to run.

It was then that he heard gunshots below and crept to the roof lantern to investigate, leaving Marie against the wall. Fearful of what he would witness he peered sheepishly down into the snooker room.

He could see Dawson ushering everyone out through the patio door with three bodies, one of them Jeremy's, lying in their wake. The others were congregating outside, unsure of what to do next.

Edward had a strong desire to call down to them, to let them know that Marie was safe, but knew that all hell was about break loose. Members of the Billingham gang were surely nearby somewhere in the grounds and to make his presence known now would put Marie in danger again. He crept back to her.

The little girl was terrified and grabbed his hand as soon as he was near enough to reach. The voices of the others, as they ran across the lawn, could be heard and then a loud thud rang out below as the library door was forced open.

Getting to the barn via the courtyard wall would be too risky now and it soon became obvious to Edward that, with the gang in pursuit of the others, going back into the house was probably his only option.

A couple of gunshots rang out somewhere down in the garden followed by more coming from some distance away. Dawson was doing his best to protect his friends as they neared the gate in the wall but was being fired on from all directions.

Their voices dwindled as they ventured further down the enclosed lawn and Edward could hear the gang members communicating as they closed in on their quarry.

He felt compelled to help them and, ordering Marie to stay put, slinked along to the edge of the roof. He could just see the last of the staff disappearing through the gate, that led to the rear of the barn. while a couple of the thugs ran towards them firing wildly.

It began to rain as Edward took aim at the moving target and, just as he squeezed the trigger, held his breath to steady the shot.

Bang! The thug fumbled to the ground and slid across the wet grass as the bullet hit. Squealing in pain he writhed on the ground. The shot was not fatal but at least it had stopped him. Edward's attention was instantly trained on the other thug.

The guy had seen the flash from the gun coming from the roof and had already stopped running. They both aimed at each other but Edward was first to fire and the thug fell lifelessly to the ground.

By now, the rest of the gang had managed to force their way into the snooker room and were already piling through the patio doors. Edward ducked away and slid back across the roof.

As quickly as he could, he removed the slats again. The guy writhing in pain was sure to give him away and he needed to get off the roof as soon as possible.

Before long they found themselves back in the twitten and Edward listened with bated breath for any signs of the person he had seen only a few minutes earlier.

Warily, he led Marie towards DaSilva's room. It would give him a clear view of both the barn and the grounds but as they neared more gunshots were heard coming from the barn.

Peering through the bars of the Juliet balcony, Edward scanned the courtyard below as he wondered how many of the gang were left. He was running low on bullets and was concerned they may outnumber his supply.

There was movement down in the courtyard, glistening wet bodies sneaking around and checking the windows for access. More movement caught his eye out on the lawn as others made their way back to the manor.

The gang had split up and they obviously knew he was still in the building. Three, may be four of them, disappeared back inside and Edward needed a plan. He began searching DaSilva's room for something he could use as one sprang to mind.

Big Dan and three of his gang stood at the foot of the stairs as they scanned the atrium above, guns poised and ready. They all knew Edward was willing to kill on site and they had to be prepared to do the same, the girl included.

They all knew that life in prison was now the best they could hope for unless they got rid of all the witnesses. Dan had been strongly against it before it had escalated into a blood bath but now found himself with no other choice. Jeremy's plan was the only one he had.

Cautiously, they made their way onto the half landing before splitting into two pairs, each taking the opposite flight. Edward had made them nervous and they all ascended sheepishly, and were all wary to peer above the head of the stairs.

Dan had chosen the flight that led to Sophia's room while the other pair, which included the skinhead with the goatee, had taken the one that led to DaSilva's. The skinhead had been here before but this time unknowingly made his way towards Edward.

As he and his partner neared the corridor with DaSilva's room at the other end they paused briefly as they prepared themselves for any sudden movement. Edward could be hiding in any of the rooms along the corridor and they edged their way forward, stopping to check each room with the bravery of a pair of quivering girls.

Suddenly, DaSilva's bedroom door burst open and a shot was fired. Startled, the jittery pair retaliated with shots of their own only to realise, too late, that they had been tricked.

With their attention on the doorway ahead, Edward emerged from one of the rooms they had already checked and blasted them from behind. He had just enough time to kill the pair before shots were fired from the other side of the atrium.

The bullets pelted the walls and doorframes, splintered wood was flying everywhere but, somehow, Edward managed to dart back to safety without being hit. He scrambled back through the vent, replaced the cover and guided Marie towards the metal ladder.

His hastily thought out plan had worked well. With Marie safely hidden in the vent of DaSilva's room she was able to pull the door open, using thick fishing twine found amongst Armando's things and attached to the door handle. The next part of her task was the frightening part but she had managed to fire Red's pistol before heading to the room Edward was now in. She had drawn their attention perfectly.

Young Kane knew Dan had seen which room he had darted into and was also aware that the big lad knew about the twitten. He was sure to send another henchman after them immediately and had to hurry.

With Marie riding piggyback again he carefully mounted the cold metal ladder but before he had began his descent they could hear someone scurrying towards them in the darkness.

Edward felt his sister's arms tighten anxiously around his neck as he began climbing down but, with Marie's added weight and not being able to see, it was more difficult than usual. He was slow and clumsy and could feel panic building up with every misjudged step.

They were still many rungs from the ground floor when a darkened figure appeared through the grainy gloom above them. Edward had to think fast and, knowing she may be hurt, he wrenched Marie's arms free with one hand and blindly lowered and flung her aside.

A split second later a shot was fired that ricocheted off the ladder in a flash of sparks followed by another and Edward lost his footing and was forced to cling on by one hand. Frightened and flustered, he tried in vain to get the gun from his satchel but then, disaster.

Another wild bullet ricocheted off the rung he was clinging to and took a finger off in the process. Edward yelped and let go, falling into the blackness.

He crumpled heavily onto the ground floor with half his body dangling down into the basement and he frantically clawed himself away as another bullet was fired.

Panic-stricken, Edward retrieved the pistol from his satchel but was forced to use his left hand to fire it. Aiming blindly, he quickly emptied a magazine before rummaging for another.

Although he had lost a finger and could hardly see through the blackness, he managed to reload the pistol quickly and continued to shoot up at the hole in the floor.

A few shots later, Edward realised that the enemy had stopped firing back and paused his own onslaught to listen. He had assumed the man had stopped to reload but could hear nothing at all. Reloading made a noise, as did any movement but, there was only dead silence above him.

Whispering, he called to Marie. He could hardly see anything until movement on the opposite side of the ladder caught his eye and he crawled towards her.

She began whimpering as he approached her and was relieved to find her relatively unharmed, shaken and scared perhaps but better than being dead. He fumbled for the sliding panel and helped her through it.

Dan had followed the gunshots back to the open vent near the stairs and was cautiously peering down through the twitten. It was too dark to see anything but had managed to work out where the last shots had come from and quickly made his down to the hall.

Standing near one of the doors to the under stairs cupboard, Dan listened for any movement. He knew there was another door on the other side of the stairs but dared not move again in case of being discovered.

Sure enough, he could hear someone moving around inside the cupboard and readied himself to react the moment the door opened but was forced to dart across the hall as they emerged from the other door.

"Stop!" Dan bawled, "or I'll shoot the girl."

The fleeing pair stopped in their tracks as the order was repeated again, reinforced with a gunshot towards them.

"Toss the gun."

Edward, bleeding from his right hand, looked at the pistol in his left as he contemplated for a second or two on spinning around to fire back but, knowing it would mean instant death for Marie if he tried, flung it aside.

Dan's nervous persona changed the moment the gun was tossed and the threat was eliminated. He approached them, chest out and confident. He was now in control and could afford to take his time.

"Turn round," he growled, gun poised.

His captives did as he asked.

Distant gunshots were heard as they stood looking at each other for a few moments. Edward with caged rage and Dan with begrudging respect for a lad that had wiped out more than half the gang single handed.

Edward pulled Marie behind him and stood staring in defiance as Dan began to smile. A thought had just crossed the big lad's mind and Edward did not like what it meant.

"Why don't you just go? he hissed. "The Billingham's are dead and you no longer have a job."

Dan's smile transformed into a vexed frown.

"I'll be going soon enough," he replied, stepping closer, "Once I've taken care of you!."

Taking another step towards Edward, Big Dan swiped the lad across the face with his pistol and followed him as he staggered sideways. Marie screamed at the sound of the attack and watched as her saviour fell.

Dazed, Edward crumpled to the ground but then felt himself being plucked to his feet before being thrown towards the stairs. He brushed against the newel post and ended up sprawled across the bottom steps.

Marie ran towards Edward but she too was sent crashing to the hall floor by a hefty swipe across the back of her head.

Stooping over his prey, Dan pressed the barrel of his pistol against Edward's temple and Marie screamed a blood curdling scream as the sound of a gunshot reverberated around the hallway.

39

Dawson ducked as another bullet smashed through the dormer window and he turned to face the others.

"We're trapped," he told them, "and I'm almost out of ammo."

Everyone had crammed into Lisa's room at the far end of the barn. They had done well to avoid being hit by the flying lead as they piled through the ground floor door, but now, they realised they had nowhere else to go.

The sound of glass being shattered downstairs stunned everyone silent and Dawson darted for the small landing. He quickly knelt and took aim as he waited for someone to appear.

Stefan followed and stood in the doorway. He'd been given one of the guns Dawson had collected and readied himself to react. The others stood silently and listened as the thugs clambered into the room below.

Sophia was now clinging to Bautista's arm, Lisa to her grandfathers and Sarah to Mrs Holland's. DaSilva stood alone on the other side of the bed, watching and thinking.

He still had a chance of survival if he played his cards right. He had been close friends with the Billingham's and most of the gang knew him well. Once this was all over he could just leave with them and disappear.

As he observed the quivering group he realised he had nothing to lose. Sophia would never forgive him, Bautista hated him and the others had never really liked him. For him, it was time to sever all ties and change sides.

With the Billingham's dead and unable to point him out as the catalyst of this bloodbath there was a real chance for him to get out of this with his life, as long as everyone else was dead, but he would need a way of showing the gang he was on their side. Slowly, he made his way towards Dawson.

However, he had only taken a few steps when the room erupted with screams as several bullets burst through the floorboards sending splinters into the air. The coward darted back behind the bed.

An order to surrender was given followed by another bullet. It was by pure luck alone that no one had been hit.

With the group huddling closer together, Bautista was forced against the sloping roof window and as his fat cheek squashed against the glass an idea for escape was born.

A few moments later, Lisa and Sarah found themselves standing on the tiles and helping to pull Sophia up through the aperture. Another warning was heard followed by another wild bullet that shattered a roof tile not far from where they were standing.

One by one, and several warning shots later, they clambered onto the roof until only DaSilva and Dawson remained inside. The grounds man had kept guard as the others escaped, firing his last bullets to prevent the gang from gaining ground.

DaSilva watched and waited. The roof only offered a way of prolonging the inevitable with no escape. He had no intention of following the others and waited, with bated breath, for his chance to prove himself worthy to the gang.

Finally, Dawson had spent his last bullet and DaSilva made his move. As the grounds man headed for the exit he sprang towards him, wrapping his arms around his neck and forcing him to the ground.

"I have him!" he bawled, excitedly, "Come up!"

"What the fuck you doing?" Dawson grimaced, struggling to wriggle free of the slimy man's hold. "Have you gone insane?"

Gripping with all his strength, DaSilva found himself riding a bucking bronco of bone and sinew as Dawson began to gain the upper hand. Before long the creak of the stair was heard as someone ascended and the struggle intensified.

Dawson knew he was about to die but was adamant that DaSilva was going with him and soon over powered the traitor. As the bedroom door burst open he manoeuvred him into an arm lock and used him as a shield.

"Don't shoot, I'm DaSilva........."

The gunshot was deafening but Dawson could

not wait to be killed and ran forward, forcing DaSilva with him. A rally of shots rang out as he neared the door and flung his captive forward ferociously.

The weight of Armando's corpse forced the gunman back onto the landing where he lost his footing and slid backwards several steps giving Dawson time to return to the window.

Stefan hastily handed him his pistol as he approached and Dawson swiped it from his grasp, spun round, and blasted the guy as he entered the room. Wasting no time, he quickly returned to the landing and managed to force someone else to run for cover.

"Is everyone ok?" he enquired, clambering onto the roof.

The silhouettes of the others against the stormy sky could be seen meandering around on the wet tiles aimlessly, precariously.

"Yes, but where do we go from here?" Stefan enquired, "there's no way down."

"Head for Edward's room and I'll try to hold them off."

"But, they might be waiting for us."

"Just do it."

Dawson crept up over the ridge tile and crouched down as he waited for someone to poke their head through the window. His gut was telling him that there were only a couple of thugs left to deal with and was hoping he had enough bullets remaining.

He glanced over at the manor house as he thought of Edward and Marie. The gang had split up in their pursuit to kill everyone and he was hoping the siblings were still alive.

Just then, and forcing him to lose his footing, random bullets began shattering the roof tiles around him and, as he clawed for balance, he dropped the gun. It clattered down the roof and fell directly into the room below.

Before he had even gained his footing an armed thug had made his way onto the roof, his pistol trained on the aging grounds man. He laughed as he looked around at everyone on the roof.

"I'm going to enjoy this," he tittered, breathless from his effort, as a second accomplice joined him on the roof.

"A game of human lemmings!"

His friend laughed as he too looked around at everyone as they tried to keep their footing. "Human lemmings," he repeated, tittering.

The first thug turned his attention to Dawson, now resting a knee on the ridge tile for support, and ordered him to jump.

"Go on," he yelled, "or I'll just blast you off."

Dawson glanced at the others. His demeanour was now that of defeat and he knew they were all going to die. He had tried his best to protect them but had only succeeded in making them easy prey.

"Fucking jump you old shit."

Accepting his fate, Dawson struggled to his

feet. The wet tiles made it more difficult, but as he turned round, he saw a flash from the balcony opposite followed instantly by a loud bang.

Dawson ducked, grabbing onto the ridge tile again and watched as the first thug disappeared off the roof. Another shot rang out and within a blink of an eye the second thug was gone.

For a few seconds everyone was in a state of panic as they struggled to work out what had happened, but then a distant voice could be heard coming from the manor.

"Is everyone ok?"

To everyone's relief, Connor was standing at the balcony with Edward and Marie at his side. With utter delight the group made their way back inside and back to the manor house.

40

A short while later everyone had congregated in the lounge to discuss their next move and how they should explain what had happened to the police.

They had all witnessed the events unfold prior to all hell breaking loose and fully understood Edward's actions leading up to it. The problem they had now was sorting out the aftermath and how it could be resolved.

Lisa, clearly still upset and exhausted, was asked to take Marie to bed before they discussed the little girls future and Sophia, reluctant to let go of her hand, feared she was about lose her.

She had already accepted that the whole thing was partly her fault but was still heartbroken when everyone else agreed.

"You're a killer and a kidnapper!" Edward snapped, the moment Marie was out of earshot. "This is all your fault and you should be the one dying in prison for it."

"I didn't kill anyone!"

"No, but you had them killed!"

Sophia shook her head, dislodging tears. "No!"

"You knew they had to be then. How else would you get away with it?"

She looked around at everyone as she dried her eyes with a handkerchief. Mixed emotions looked back at her, pity, hate, bewilderment.

"I know what I did is unforgivable," she snivelled, "and believe me, I hate myself for it, but once Armando had Heather captive it had already gone too far."

"Don't make this out to be DaSilva's idea!" Edward retorted, "How would he have known my mom was pregnant if you hadn't told him."

Sophia struggled to reply for a moment before turning away from Edward, ashamed. The lad was right. She was still trying to deny full responsibility and was desperate to lessen her involvement.

"You signed her death warrant you evil bitch!"

Bautista called for calm as he struggled to clamber out from the low soft sofa he had chosen. There was a pause as everyone bar Edward watched the portly man struggle to his feet.

"May I propose a solution," he huffed, straightening his shirt.

"As long as it means she goes to prison and I leave with Marie!" Edward snapped, still glaring at Mrs Carter.

"But, young man, Marie will end up the bigger victim in all this." Bautista added, "if you also end up behind bars "

Edward listened without reply. He felt that the blood on his hands was justified but knew what the fat man was getting at. He was no longer an innocent victim but a cold bloodied killer. He had not even given the corpses he had left in his wake a single thought until now.

It was then that Connor interjected.

"In Edward's defence," he said, lighting a cigarette, "it was self-defence."

"Tell that to their families," Bautista remarked, glancing briefly at the chauffeur, "They'll want answers, and they'll want justice."

"I want justice!" Edward barked, "She's a monster!"

"But to Marie, she's her mother."

"Then what do you suggest?" Sarah asked, now comforting Albert in Lisa's absence.

"For Marie' sake, I suggest we come up with a plan that prevents anyone from going to prison."

Edward scoffed, "No fucking way!"

"Now listen to me Edward. I know you won't like it but, Marie is likely to end up in care if you leave now. You'd be a fugitive and, once caught, be jailed for life alongside Sophia."

Edward looked around at the bedraggled group for signs of support, a reassuring smile perhaps or a knowing nod, but none came. He had dragged them through hell and back and did feel sorry for that but, would they point him out as the bad guy in all this?

As if reading his mind, Bautista continued.

"We all know where the real blame lies but this situation needn't have happened if you'd have handled it differently."

Edward huffed.

"I was going to call the police the moment

that slimy bastard confessed but the Billingham's turned up," he hissed, "I was handling it just fine."

"You should've just gone to the police. If you had, the manor wouldn't be littered with bodies right now would it?"

"No, but she and DaSilva would still be going to prison wouldn't they?"

There was a pause as Edward and Bautista looked at each other. They both had valid points but young Kane had to admit, the bloodshed could have been avoided.

As the pair stood and looked at each other Connor poured himself a drink before asking Bautista what he had in mind. The chauffeur had also killed this evening and if there was a way for him to get away with it he was all ears.

"I'm not entirely sure," the fat man began, making his way towards Connor and pouring himself a drink. Everyone watched in silence.

"A business deal gone bad or a quarrel over the upcoming contest," he explained, pausing to sip his brandy. "It can be whatever we decide but, we need a fall guy, someone to blame."

"Someone dead." Connor added.

Bautista nodded.

"The place is littered with Billingham's and their army of thugs. I suggest we put the blame squarely with them. We can say that we were simply caught up in a personal vendetta that spiralled out of control."

He glanced around at his tired and dishevelled

audience for approval before taking another sip of brandy.

"We just need to agree a story and stick to it," he added.

"Then what?" Edward asked, shrugging his shoulders, "What happens to everyone after that. She gets away with killing my parents, keeps Marie and we all walk away as if nothing's happened?

"No, no my boy. Everything goes on as before."

"How?"

"Well, Sophia keeps the manor, Marie keeps a roof over her head, everyone keeps their positions - with bonuses of course - and I teach you how to run the company with the help of Connor here."

"What? And live here with her?"

"Either that or the orphanage for Marie and prison for you!"

Before Edward had time to reply, Sarah stood up and agreed with the plan, gesturing to the others to comply.

"It sounds like the best option we have," she offered.

"I want Marie to know who she is."

"Perhaps in time, Edward," Bautista replied, turning to his sister, "when she's old enough to understand."

Sophia, face smeared with tears and make-up, nodded back at him.

"The manor is big enough for you two to hardly meet and eventually, my boy, you and your sister will inherit the lot."

Edward, stunned into silence, gawped back at the portly man.

"What do you say?" Bautista added.

MORE TITLES BY PAUL J JACKSON

'My Soul to Take' - After being saved from certain death, Amelia is plunged into a nightmare that involves her husband, a woman named Kate and an army of subterranean demons hell bent on war. With the help of a renegade demon, she embarks on a perilous journey that is fraught with danger, betrayal and death.

'Down a Dark Path' - (Sinister Tales of Supernatural Horror) -
A murderer gets more than he bargained for - An innocent man tries to cheat death against a sinister demon - A man down on his luck sees an opportunity to turn his fortunes around but soon wishes he hadn't - A bogus reporter meets an old man with a terrifying tale - Taking a short cut home proves to be a grave mistake for Blake - While waiting to die, Nate recalls the time he tried to alter fate that had disastrous consequences - While surveying an abandoned building, William is sucked into a ghostly nightmare - A desperate warrior embarks on a perilous journey to find sanctuary only to end up fighting for his life.

'Retribution' - A spate of gruesome murders has DI Lockwood baffled until he receives a letter that points to an unsolved missing persons case that is somehow connected. As he rounds up the suspects mentioned in the unsolved case, it soon becomes clear that something more sinister is at play and is killing those involved. As the body count rises, Lockwood closes in but no one is prepared for what happens next.

ABOUT THE AUTHOR

Paul J Jackson lives in the West Midlands, England, with his wife, two daughters and his beloved border collie.

His preferred genre is supernatural horror but his stories are varied, ranging from horror to crime thrillers, from fantasy to the unusual.

When he's not writing stories he enjoys entering writing competitions and has been published in the Oxford Flash Fiction Antholgy titled 'Sticks and Stones' with his story 'The Lover', and in the Retreat West Anthology after being short listed in their short story competition with 'The Leonids'

He is featured on

Charlie

Printed in Great Britain
by Amazon

82309636R00171